THE TWO LOOKED AT EACH OTHER IN SILENCE.

Original illustration from the 1900 David C. Cook printing of Charles Sheldon's classic
Robert Hardy's Seven Days. Illustrator unknown.

Robert Hardy's Seven Days

Robert Hardy's Seven Days

CHARLES SHELDON

RIVEROAK®

Good News in Fiction

COOK COMMUNICATIONS MINISTRIES
Colorado Springs, Colorado • Paris, Ontario
KINGSWAY COMMUNICATIONS LTD
Eastbourne, England

RiverOak® is an imprint of
Cook Communications Ministries, Colorado Springs, CO 80918
Cook Communications, Paris, Ontario
Kingsway Communications, Eastbourne, England

ROBERT HARDY'S SEVEN DAYS
© 2007 by Cook Communications Ministries
Originally printed in 1900 by David C. Cook Publishing. This edition is copyright © 2007 by Cook Communications Ministries.

Cover Design: Amy Kiechlin

Printed in the United States of America

ISBN 978-1-58919-080-1

REV. CHARLES M. SHELDON.

Author portrait from the 1900 David C. Cook printing of Charles Sheldon's classic *Robert Hardy's Seven Days*. Photographer/engraver unknown.

PUTTING FAITH INTO ACTION

CHARLES MONROE Sheldon—pastor, famous author, and tireless reformer—was a man who viewed Christian ministry and social activism as intertwined and inseparable. Contrary to many theologians of his day who regarded the practical ills of society as irrelevant to the task of winning souls, Sheldon believed Christianity would be considered irrelevant if it made no attempt to meet people's real needs and relieve suffering in tangible ways.

Near the end of his astonishing career, Sheldon was asked by seminary students to share his "tenets of ministry." He began as a pastor, he replied, with an "unquestioning faith in Jesus Christ as the one and only power in all the world, and the only one capable of saving the world." After more than thirty years of activist ministry, during which time he published thirty novels—including the classic *In His Steps*, one of the best-selling books of all time—it was clear that "saving the world" meant far more to Sheldon than an abstract theological concept.

"I define my Christ," he continued, "as the greatest statesman and economist of all time, and insist that legislation and education and political economy and industry look to Him as the one ... holding in His teaching the redemption of the world at every point."

In other words, Sheldon never saw a need or problem in the world that could not be remedied by the application of Christ's simplest teachings.

"Think on this," he wrote. "If men sought first the kingdom of God through Jesus Christ, they would have all the other material things necessary for human happiness."[1]

Sheldon's views reflected a larger movement of the time called "Christian Socialism." Although the word *socialism* would take on negative connotations in succeeding decades, at that time it meant addressing society's and individuals' needs and seeking practical ways to relieve hardship. Adherents of the movement emphasized leading a Christlike life and *doing* things to help people in Jesus' name.

Walter Rauschenbusch, a leader of the movement who credited *In His Steps* as his greatest influence, wrote that Christ died to "substitute love for selfishness as the basis of human society."[2] That idea is the common thread that runs through Charles Sheldon's legacy of ministry and literature.

The great social upheaval of the latter decades of the 1800s—when Sheldon began his ministry—provided fertile ground for advocates of Christian Socialism. In the United States, the wounds of the Civil War were still fresh, and the country had to contend with the northward and westward migration of former slaves in search of a better life. Steel, petroleum, and electricity had propelled the Industrial Revolution, fueling massive change as factories drew workers from the countryside into rapidly expanding cities. Divisions between rich and poor stood in sharp contrast, and the labor movement was a powerful and unstable force confronting unfair and unsafe working conditions. Immigration altered the face of the nation, seemingly on a daily basis.

These issues all found their way into Sheldon's novels and influenced his philosophy of "untheological Christianity."[3] He believed that talking about God's love and grace without doing something to demonstrate them represented a shallow, hollow kind of faith. He consistently and unflinchingly brought these issues to life through his characters. Sheldon biographer Ellen Caughey wrote,

> Charles's novels, like other popular "social gospel" literature of the era, contained common themes. They were tributes to the middle-class working man, caught between the simpler days of rural living and the impending industrial modernization of the twentieth century. The differences between the rich and the poor, labor management and the struggling factory workers, and those who frequented barrooms and who were faithful churchgoers were emphasized. But his novels were filled with optimism, too. The future always looked bright whenever the protagonist decided to follow God's way and seek solutions found in the Bible.[4]

Sheldon's upbringing inspired him and prepared him to address themes involving the collision of rural and urban life as well as a moral versus immoral lifestyle. Born in 1857 to a Congregational minister and his wife, Sheldon moved with his family often during the first ten years of his life. The family finally settled down in 1867, when his father was named the Home Missionary Superintendent for the Dakota Territory, encompassing modern-day North and South Dakota. The family moved to a 160-acre homestead on the wide-open prairie outside Yankton. Indians were often seen camping in tepees at the edge of the family's property.

For young Charles, it was a life of adventure and hard work. All five Sheldon children shared equally in the task of running a frontier household isolated from civilization. Years later he wrote, "If there was anything that Dakota farm taught us all for life, it was the dignity and joy of work with our hands."[5]

Sheldon also learned to delight in using his mind and imagination. The need to provide one's own entertainment on the prairie created in him a lifelong love of books. At the end of each day, he could be found at the kitchen table with a kerosene lantern and his latest book, borrowed from a generous family friend in Yankton. He read Sir Walter Scott, Dickens, and Shakespeare. The family also read the Bible aloud each morning, starting over at Genesis every time they reached the end of Revelation.

Inspired by such a rich literary environment, Sheldon began writing stories of his own. By the time he left his prairie home to attend school in Andover, Massachusetts, several of his tales had been published in the Yankton newspaper, and he had even sold one to an East Coast magazine. On one trip to Boston as a student, Charles found a copy of *Les Miserables* in a bookshop he visited often. Without hesitation he bought the book, spending the money he needed for return train fare to Andover. After using his last few coins for a sandwich and a cup of coffee, he walked twenty miles back to campus in a drizzling rain. His prize, however, remained dry, tucked away in his shirt.

After graduating from Andover Theological Seminary in 1886, Sheldon accepted the pastorate of the Congregational church in Waterbury, Vermont. There, he was determined to be the perfect example of what New Englanders expected in a minister. But it was there that he began to develop his conviction that Christian ministry must consist of action rather than mere spiritual theorizing. When he saw a need, he was compelled to do everything he could to meet it, even if his efforts had nothing to do with traditional evangelism.

For instance, it came to Sheldon's attention that many of the ladies in Waterbury complained about the amount of dust created by traffic on the town's dirt streets. It infiltrated their homes through open windows and coated the furniture. He went to work immediately and organized the construction of a pipeline from a nearby spring to a holding tank in town. Then he conscripted a townsman to drive a water wagon that sprinkled the roads to control the dust. A huge crowd turned out for the inaugural voyage down Main Street, and for the remainder of his time in Waterbury, Sheldon had devoted supporters among the members of the Ladies Aid Society.

Another time, Sheldon and a local physician conducted a study that linked a string of mysterious deaths in the town to contaminated drinking water where pig stalls were placed too close to wells. He also organized a church garden that became a profitable source of funds for the needy and for missions. He created a popular reading club for the town's young people, "something for them to do besides dancing and card-playing."[6] Sheldon went on to found the town's first library.

As much as Sheldon's time in Waterbury had done to shape his Christian Socialist theology, the town would play an equally large role in the young minister's personal life. It was there he met Mary "May" Merriam, whom he married in 1891. The couple would eventually have one child together, a son.

May's father facilitated Sheldon's move to the pastorate of a new Congregational church in Topeka, Kansas. Indeed, Sheldon was eager to return to the prairie of his childhood where the breezes, he wrote, "start somewhere in the Rocky Mountains and do not stop until they hit the Alleghenies, and begin to get discouraged only about the time they reach the New York Palisades."[7]

Sheldon wound up staying in Topeka for the next fifty-seven years. In 1889, at the inauguration of the Central Congregational Church building, he set the stage for his extraordinary ministry, declaring that the church would reveal "a Christ for the common people." Christ's religion, he said, "does not consist alone in cushioned seats, and comfortable surroundings, or culture, or fine singing or respectable orders of Sunday services, but [in] a Christ who bids us all recognize the Brotherhood of the race, who bids throw open this room to all."[8]

Along with his passion for ministry, Sheldon maintained his love for literature, particularly for writing stories of his own. In Topeka, he found a way to bring these two strands of his life together. Searching for a strategy to boost flagging attendance at Sunday evening services, he remembered the popularity of the book club he'd founded in Waterbury. He made a decision that was to shape his literary career for the rest of his life and even lead him to write *In His Steps*. Sheldon decided that, instead of preaching on Sunday evenings, he would write novels and read new chapters aloud each week. His first book—*Richard Bruce, or the Life That Now Is*—was an unqualified success, drawing ever-larger crowds, along with offers from publishers to print his stories.

If Sheldon's writing seems to be overtly instructive and moralistic to modern readers, there's a good reason: Virtually every novel and short story he wrote was first and foremost a sermon delivered from his pulpit. If readers in our more skeptical era find his tone "preachy," it is because he literally preached his material before adapting it to print form.

Whatever the criticisms about his writing, the strategy worked wonders. By all accounts, his parishioners found his spoken-word stories and parables thoroughly captivating. For Sheldon, this formula allowed him—and forced him—to produce at least one chapter each week, which added up to a novel or two each year. It was a method Sheldon employed to great effect for decades.

Meanwhile, Sheldon wasted no time making good

on his promise to "throw open the doors" in his ministry. He announced a plan to identify eight sections of his city and then spend a week living among each of them, learning firsthand the needs of common people. Over the following two months, he immersed himself in the world of streetcar operators, college students, impoverished blacks, railroad workers, lawyers, physicians, businessmen, and newspaper workers.

The weeks spent among the African Americans in Tennesseetown—as the segregated section of Topeka was known—were to be the most important to Sheldon, giving shape to a new mission for his church. During subsequent years, he spearheaded numerous outreach projects among the thousand or so freed slaves living in Tennesseetown. There, he founded one of the first kindergartens in the country, a school that became a model for others across the nation. Furthermore, his church provided job training, established a library, led efforts to close down saloons and "speakeasies," created village beautification programs, planted new churches, and opened its own doors to black members (quite progressive and controversial at the time).

Sheldon wrote of these experiences in his novel *The Redemption of Freetown*. Fictional pastor Howard Douglass said,

How shall we redeem Freetown? It is not an

impossibility. It is not a vague dream of what may be. It is within the reach of actual facts.... The place can be saved. But it is God's way to save men by means of other men. He does not save by means of angels, or in any way apart from the use of men as the means.

Throughout his career, Sheldon was a vocal opponent of drinking, gambling, greed, corruption, and misuse of the Sabbath. Nearly all of his books—which were often autobiographical—confront these evils and place the burden of responsibility for social reform squarely on Christians. For instance, *Miracle at Markham* is partly set in Pyramid, Colorado, a rowdy mining town with a gambling problem. A young minister, Francis Randall, is determined to stamp the evil out.

There were two sentences in [Francis Randall's] sermon near the close that struck William's mind like a blow: "Any Christian living in Pyramid today is a coward and is faithless if he does not do all in his power to confront this gambling curse. No one has any right to say it is none of his business."

To Sheldon, the whole point of Christianity was to lead a Christlike life, which he saw as the foundation of the kingdom of God on earth. He was impatient with anything less. To him, addressing poverty, injustice, vice, and wasteful living were not distractions from saving souls; confronting these and other issues represented a Christian's first calling.

This conviction led him to write the most influential four words of his entire career: What would Jesus do?

The novel *In His Steps: What Would Jesus Do?*—which would go on to sell more than thirty million copies worldwide—began like his other books, as episodes to be read on Sunday nights. In the story, Reverend Henry Maxwell faces a crisis when he fails to help a tramp who comes to his door asking for work in the church. Maxwell politely turns him away, "too busy" to do anything more. The following Sunday morning, the tramp shows up at Maxwell's church and makes another appeal, this time in public.

"It seems to me," the man says to the assembled congregation, "there's an awful lot of trouble in the world that somehow wouldn't exist if all the people who sing such songs went and lived them out."

Maxwell is stunned. He takes the man home with him, only to watch him die a few days later. Stricken with guilt at the man's rebuke, Maxwell makes this plea the following Sunday to his congregation:

The appearance and words of this stranger in the

church last Sunday made a very powerful impression on me. I am not able to conceal from you or myself the fact that what he said, followed as it has been by his death in my house, has compelled me to ask as I never asked before, "What does following Jesus mean?" ... What I am going to propose now ... ought not to appear unusual or at all impossible.... I want volunteers from the First Church who will pledge themselves, earnestly and honestly for an entire year, not to do anything without first asking the question, "What would Jesus do?" And after asking that question, each one will follow Jesus as exactly as he knows how, no matter what the result may be.

The story follows those who answer this call and details the difficulties they face and the sacrifices they must accept. It is an indictment of the compromises Christians make in the world of politics and commerce that often directly lead to suffering and injustice in the lives of common people.

The Sunday night readings of *In His Steps*, like Sheldon's other stories, were a huge hit. Word of the book quickly reached the Advance Publishing Company in Chicago. The editors wrote to Sheldon offering seventy-five dollars for the rights to publish the story in serial form. Sheldon accepted the offer, despite advice from family members that he should seek out a company willing to publish the chapters altogether as a complete book. The immediate and overwhelming success of the series surprised everyone, perhaps the Advance Publishing Company most of all. In the rush to get the first issues to print, the company neglected to file the proper copyright paperwork.

It was soon discovered that Sheldon no longer held the legal rights to *In His Steps*. As a result, dozens of publishers hurried to the printers with their own versions, and Sheldon received little remuneration from the sales. The book could have made him a millionaire, but he never grew bitter about his lost fortune. Years later, he wrote, "The very fact that over fifty different publishers put the book out gave it a wide reading, and established its public as no other one publisher could possibly have done."[9] Before his death in 1946, Sheldon had seen the book translated into thirty-two foreign languages.

In 1912, after twenty-four years in the pulpit, Sheldon resigned as pastor of Central Congregational Church. Over the next several years, he crisscrossed the country and traveled the world as part of a vigorous campaign to promote the national prohibition of alcohol. He returned to his pastorate in Topeka briefly after the Eighteenth Amendment to the Constitution was ratified, but in 1919 he retired from the church for good. For several years thereafter, he was editor-in-chief of *Christian Herald* magazine. Never one to be idle, Sheldon remained active during his retirement years, writing, speaking, traveling, and participating in numerous ministry endeavors. He died in 1946, two days short of his eighty-ninth birthday.

Almost a half century later, Sheldon's words swept the United States again when *In His Steps* and its message of uncompromised Christian duty unexpectedly regained widespread popularity. Before long, "WWJD?" (short for "What Would Jesus Do?") showed up on countless T-shirts, bracelets, key chains, bumper stickers, bookmarks, and trinkets of every kind. One can only speculate about how Sheldon would have reacted to such a phenomenon. Would he have been pleased that his phrase piqued interest and prompted people to think about their actions? Or would he have lamented the commercialization of a genuine, heartfelt question for people of faith?

Whatever the case, Sheldon's words, spoken through his protagonist Henry Maxwell, seem more urgent today than ever:

The call of this dying century and of the new one soon to be, is a call for a new discipleship, a new following of Jesus, more like the early, simple, apostolic Christianity, when the disciples left all and literally followed the Master. Nothing but a discipleship of this kind can face the destructive selfishness of the age with any hope of overcoming it.

Charles Sheldon preached and wrote about the world-changing power of the Christlike life. His greatest achievement is the proof he offered—in himself—that such a life is possible.

Notes

1. Ellen Caughey, *Charles Sheldon* (Uhrichsville, OH: Barbour Publishing, 2000), 189–90.

2. "The Theology and Writings of Walter Rauschenbusch," Georgetown College course syllabus, ed. Kyle Potter, http://spider.georgetowncollege.edu/htallant/courses/his338/students/kpotter/writings.htm.

3. Timothy Miller, *Following In His Steps* (Knoxville: University of Tennessee Press, 1987), 187.

4. Caughey, *Sheldon*, 111.

5. Miller, *Following In His Steps*, 7.

6. Caughey, *Sheldon*, 55.

7. Ibid., 184.

8. Miller, *Following In His Steps*, 23.

9. Ibid., 99.

1

A Hardened Heart

Reaping That Which Was Sown

**I**T WAS SUNDAY NIGHT, AND Robert Hardy had just come home from the evening service in the church at Barton. He was not in the habit of attending the evening service, but something said by his minister that morning had compelled him to go.

The evening had been a little unpleasant and a light snow was falling. Robert's wife, Mary, had excused herself from going to church on that account. Robert came home cross and faultfinding.

"You won't catch me going to evening service again!" he grumbled. "Only fifty people there, and it was a sheer waste of fuel and light. The sermon was one of the dullest I ever heard. I believe Reverend Jones is growing too old for our church. We need a young man, more up with the times. Jones is forever harping on the necessity of doing what we can to save souls. To hear him talk, you would think every man who wasn't running around to save souls was a robber and an enemy of society. He keeps going on, too, about this newfangled 'Christian Socialism,' as he calls it. He thinks rich men are oppressing the poor and that church members need to take more literally the teachings of Christ about helping the underprivileged. Bah! I am sick of being harangued about helping the needy. I'll withdraw my tithe pledge if the present style of preaching continues."

Mary waited patiently until her husband's outburst had subsided. Then she asked, "What was the text of the sermon tonight?"

"Oh, I don't remember exactly," Robert said. "Something about 'This night thy soul shall be demanded,' or words to that effect. I don't believe in this attempt to scare folks into heaven."

"It would take a good many sermons to scare you, Robert," Mary chided.

"Yes, more than two a week," he replied with a dry laugh. He took off his overcoat and settled into the sofa in front of the open fire. He seemed to be listening for something for a few moments, and then asked, "Where are the girls?"

"Alice is upstairs reading the morning paper," she answered. "Clara and Bess went over to visit the Caxtons."

"How did they happen to go over there?"

Mary hesitated. Finally, she said, "James came over and invited them."

"They know I have forbidden them to have anything to do with the Caxtons!" Robert nearly shouted. "When they come back, I will let them know I mean what I say. It is very strange that the girls don't appear to understand that."

Robert rose from the sofa and walked across the room, then came back and sat down again. From this position, he poked the fire brusquely with the shovel. Mary bit her lip and seemed on the point of replying, but she said nothing.

At last Robert asked, "And where are the boys?"

"Will is studying up in his room. George went

out about eight o'clock. He didn't say where he was going."

"Isn't this a nice family!" Robert's tone dripped with sarcasm. "Is there one night in the year, Mary, when all our children are at home?"

"Almost as many as there are when *you* are at home," Mary retorted. "What with your club and your lodge and your scientific society and your reading group and your directors' meeting, the children see about as much of you as you do of them. How many nights in a week do you give us, Robert? Do you think it is strange that the children go out to socialize and have fun? Our home—" Mary paused and looked around at the costly interior of the room where the two were. "Our home is well furnished with everything but our own children!"

The man on the sofa was silent. He felt the sharpness of the thrust made by his wife and knew it was too true to be denied. But Robert was, above all other things, selfish. He had not the remotest intention of giving up his club or his scientific society or his frequent cozy dinners with businessmen downtown just because his wife spent so many lonely evenings at home and because his children were almost strangers to him.

Still, it annoyed him, as a respectable citizen, to have his children making friends with people he did not approve of, and it grated on his old-fashioned, inherited New England ideas that his boys and girls should be away from home so often in the evening, and especially on Sunday evening.

The maxim of Robert Hardy's life was "self-interest first." As long as he was not thwarted in his own pleasures, he was as good-natured and pleasant as the next man. He provided liberally for the household expenses, and his wife and children were supplied with money and the means to travel as they requested it. But the minute he was crossed in his own plans, or anyone demanded of him a service that compelled some sacrifice, he became hard, ill-natured, and haughty.

He had been a member of the church at Barton for twenty-five years, one of the trustees, and a generous giver. He prided himself on that fact. But so far as giving any of his time or personal service was concerned, he would as soon have thought of giving all his property away to the first poor man he met.

Reverend Jones had the previous week written Robert an earnest, warmhearted letter expressing much pleasure at the service he had rendered so many years as a trustee, and asking him to come to the Wednesday evening meeting that week to participate and help out. Robert had read the letter through hastily and smiled a little scornfully. He could not remember when he had attended a Wednesday prayer meeting—they were too dull for him. He wondered at the pastor for writing such a letter and almost felt as though he had been impertinent. He threw the letter in the wastebasket and did not bother to answer it. He would not have been guilty of such a lack of courtesy in regard to a business letter, but correspondence from his minister was another thing. The idea of replying to a letter from him never occurred to Robert. And when Wednesday night came, he went downtown to a meeting of the chess club and had a good time with his favorite game. He was, after all, a fine chess player and engaged in a series of games that were being played for the state championship.

Then there was the other request for Robert's time and energy. The superintendent of the Sunday school had timidly approached Robert and asked if he would teach a boys' class. What? Teach a bunch of squirrelly, rambunctious boys? He, the influential, wealthy manager of one of the largest railroad enterprises in the world? He, give his time to the teaching of a Sunday school class?

He excused himself because of "lack of time," and the very same evening of his conversation with the superintendent, he went to the theater and later, after he got home, puttered in the chemistry laboratory in the attic of his house. Anything that gave him pleasure, Robert was willing to work for. He was not lazy; but the idea of giving his personal time, service, and talents to bless the world had no place in his mind.

So, as he lay on the sofa that evening and listened to his wife's plain statement concerning his selfishness, he had no intention of giving up a single thing that gratified his tastes and fed his pride.

After a long silence, Mary said coldly, as if it were a matter of indifference to her, "Mr. Burns called while you were out."

That the foreman of Robert's railroad shop had inquired of him at home was unusual.

"He did?" Robert said. "What did he want?"

"He said four of the men in the casting room were severely injured this afternoon in an accident,"

Mary explained. "The entire force quit work and went home."

"Well, couldn't Burns replace the injured men? He knows where to find replacements."

Mary shrugged. "That's what he came to see you about. He said he needed further directions. The men flatly refused to work another minute and all left together. I can't say I blame them." She paused for a moment, then asked, "Robert, do you think it's right to keep the factory open on Sunday?"

"What? Be realistic, Mary," replied Robert, though with a shadow of uneasiness in his tone. "This is a full-time operation. It is a demanding work and vital to transportation, business, and the economy. Railroad workers are public servants; they can't rest Sundays."

"So I guess when God instructed people not to work on Sundays, he didn't mean railroad workers?" Mary replied. "The Fourth Commandment ought to read, 'Remember the Sabbath day and keep it holy, except all you men who work for railroads. You haven't any Sunday.'"

Robert folded his arms. "Mary, I didn't come from one sermon to listen to another. You're worse than Reverend Jones."

He shifted his weight on the sofa and leaned on his elbow, glaring at his wife with obvious displeasure on his face. Yet, as he looked, he remembered his old New England home back in the Vermont hills, and the vision of that quiet little country village where Mary and he had grown up together. He saw the old meetinghouse on the hill, at the end of a long, elm-shaded street that straggled through the village. He saw himself again as he began to fall in love with Mary and remembered the Sunday when, walking back from church by Mary's side, he had asked her to be his wife. It seemed to him that a breeze from the meadow beyond Squire Hazen's place swirled around him, just as it had when Mary turned and said the happy word making that day the gladdest, proudest day he had ever known. What memories of the old times! What—

He started and came out of his reverie. He looked into the fire as if wondering where he was, not noticing the tear that rolled down his wife's cheek and fell on her hands clasped in her lap. Mary arose and went over to the piano, which stood in the shadows. Sitting down with her back to her husband, she played fragments of music nervously. Robert lay down on the sofa again.

After a while, Mary turned on the piano stool and said, "Robert, don't you think you should go over and see Mr. Burns about the men who are hurt?"

"Why, what can I do about it? The company's doctor will see to them. I would only be in the way. Did Burns say if they were badly hurt?"

"Yes, very badly," Mary said. "It seems as though one of them will be permanently blinded, and another will lose both feet. I think he said the man's name was Scoville."

Robert sat up immediately. "What? Not Ward Scoville?"

"I'm certain that's the name Burns mentioned."

Robert rose from the sofa, then lay down again. "Oh, well, I can go there the first thing in the morning. I can't do anything now."

But there came to his mind a picture of when he was walking through the machine shops one day. A heavy piece of casting had broken from the end of a large hoisting derrick and would have fallen on him and probably killed him if Scoville, at the time a workman in the machine department, had not pulled him to one side, at the risk of his own life. As it was, Scoville was struck on the shoulder and rendered unable to work for four weeks. Robert had raised his wages and promoted him to a more responsible position in the casting room.

Robert was not a man without generosity and humane feeling. But as he lay on the couch and thought of the cold snow outside and the distance to the shop tenements, he readily excused himself from going out to see the man who had once saved his life—a man who now lay desperately injured.

Mary, who rarely ventured to oppose her husband's wishes, again turned to the piano and struck a few chords aimlessly. Then she wheeled about and said abruptly, "I almost forgot. Natalie told me she has to leave us and go home at once. She's been a wonderful cook and a great help—I hate to lose her."

Robert had begun to doze a little, but at this sudden announcement he sat up and exclaimed, "Well, you are the bearer of bad news tonight. What's the matter with everybody? I suppose the girl wants more pay?"

Mary replied quietly, "Her sister is dying. And do you know, I believe I have never given the girl credit for enough feeling. She always seemed to me a bit cold, though she is certainly the most faithful and efficient servant we ever had in the house. She came in just after Mr. Burns left, and broke down, crying bitterly. It seems her sister is married to one of the railroad men here in town and has been seriously ill for months. She is very poor, and her family struggles to survive. Natalie was almost beside herself with grief as she told the story. She said she must go and care for her sister, who probably won't live more than a week. I pitied the poor girl. Robert, don't you think we could do something for the family? We have so much. We could easily help them and not miss a single thing."

"And where would such help end?" Robert replied. "If we give to every needy person who comes along, we will have beggars lining up at the door. We might become beggars ourselves. Besides, I can't afford it. The boys are a heavy expense to me while they are in college, and the company has been cutting down salaries lately. If the cook's sister is married to a railroad man, he is probably getting good wages and can support her all right."

"What if that railroad man were injured and made a cripple for life?" asked Mary.

"Then the insurance companies or charities can help them out. I don't see how we can care for every needy person who comes along. There would be no end of it."

"As nearly as I can find out," continued Mary, without replying to her husband's remarks, "Natalie's sister is married to one of the men who was hurt this afternoon. She speaks our language so poorly that I couldn't understand it all, and she was quite emotional. Suppose it was Scoville—couldn't you do something for them then, Robert?"

"I might," he replied. "But I tell you I have more demands for money now than I can meet. The church expenses, for example. Why, every week we are called on to give to some cause or other, beyond our regular pledges. It's a constant drain. I shall have to cut down on my pledge. We can't be giving to every little thing all the time and still have anything for ourselves."

Robert spoke with a touch of indignation. His wife glanced around the almost palatial room, and her face grew stern and almost forbidding as she remembered that only last week Robert had spent a hundred and fifty dollars for new equipment for his laboratory. And now he was talking as if times were hard!

Again she turned to the piano and played a while, but she was not soothed by the music. When she finally arose and walked over to the table near the end of the sofa, she realized Robert was asleep. Mary sat down and gazed into the open fire, a look of sorrow and unrest on her face. She sat like this for a half hour and was at last aroused by the two girls, Clara and Bess, coming in. They were laughing and talking together and had evidently parted with someone at the door.

Mary hurried into the hallway. "Hush, girls! Your father is asleep! You know how he hates being awakened by a sudden noise. He was waiting up for you but then dozed off."

"Then I guess we'll go upstairs without saying good night," said Clara abruptly. "I don't want to be lectured about going over to the Caxtons' house."

"No, I want to see you both and have a little talk with you. Come in here." Mary took the two girls into the front room. "Now tell me, girls, why did your father forbid you from going over to the Caxtons'? I did not know of it until tonight. Does it have something to do with James?"

Neither of the girls said anything for a minute. Then Bess, who was the younger of the two and known for startling the family with sensational remarks, replied: "James and Clara are engaged, and they are going to be married tomorrow!"

Mary looked at Clara, who grew very red in the face, and then to the surprise of her mother and Bess, the girl burst out into a violent fit of crying. She gathered the girl into her arms to quiet her, as she had when Clara was a little child.

"Tell me all about it, dear. I did not know you cared for James in that way."

"But I do!" sobbed Clara. "And Father guessed something and insisted we should never go there anymore. But I didn't think he would mind it if Bess and I went just this one night. I couldn't help it, anyway. Mother, isn't it right for people to love each other?"

"Of course it is," Mary said. But, Clara, you're still very young. And so is James."

"He's twenty-one and I'm eighteen. He's one of the best stenographers in the state and earns a decent salary. We've talked it over, and I wish we could be married tomorrow!"

Bess remarked quietly, "Yes, they've thought it through, and I think James is nice. But when I marry, I'll want a husband who makes more than a 'decent' salary. I'll want plenty of spending money. And besides, I wouldn't say James is particularly handsome."

"He is handsome!" cried Clara. "And he's good and brave, and I'd rather have him than a thousand other men! Mother, I don't care about money. It certainly hasn't made you happy."

"Hush, dear!" Mary felt as if she'd been struck in the face, and she fell silent.

Clara put her arms around her mother and whispered, "I'm sorry, Mother! I didn't mean to hurt you. But I am so unhappy!"

Mary was on the point of a reply when she heard a sound in the hallway outside, and her oldest daughter, Alice, entered the room. She was handicapped, the result of a childhood accident, and she carried a crutch, using it with much skill and even grace.

The minute Alice entered, she saw something was happening, but she simply said, "Mother, isn't it a little strange that Father fell asleep so early? Usually at this time, he's reading up in the study and working in his lab. Maybe he's ill."

"Maybe he is," said Mary as she rose and went into the other room. "I'll go check on him."

Just then the youngest boy, Will, came downstairs, carrying one of his books.

"Hey, Alice, translate this passage for me, will you?" he said. "Who cares about the old Romans anyway? What do I care about the way they fought their battles and built their one-horse bridges! What makes me angry is the way Caesar has of telling a thing. Why can't he drive straight ahead instead of beating about the bush so much?"

Will handed the book to Alice, who began to read. The boy sat down beside Bess and began to tease her and Clara.

"What are you and Clara doing at this time of day? Time you youngsters were going upstairs. Play us a little tune, Bessie, will you?" He looked at Clara and said, "It looks like you've been crying. What's the matter?"

"None of your business," she replied sharply.

"I bet it has to do with James Caxton," he chided. "Am I right?"

Going over to where Clara lay with her face hid in the cushions of a large couch, Will tried to pull the pillow out from under her head.

"Leave me alone, Will!" Clara said with a voice muffled by the pillow. "I don't feel well."

"C'mon, you're faking," he said.

"No, I'm not. Leave me alone."

Finally, Alice intervened. "Come here, Will, or I won't read your sentence for you."

Will reluctantly left Clara, for he knew from experience that Alice would keep her word.

At that moment, the door opened and in walked George, the older boy, and the eldest of all the children. He hung up his hat and coat and strolled into the room.

"Where's Mother?"

"She's in the other room," answered Bess. "Father's been asleep, and she was afraid he's gotten sick."

"That's one of your stories," said George, who seemed in a good-natured mood. He sat down and drew his little sister toward him and whispered to her, "Say, Bess, I need some money."

"Again?" whispered Bess. "What for this time?"

"Well … for a special reason. Do you think you could let me have a little?"

"I suppose. I've got my month's allowance. But why don't you ask Father?"

"I've asked him too much lately," George said. "He refused point-blank last time. I didn't like the way he spoke."

"Well, you can have all mine," said Bess, still whispering.

George and she were very close, and there was not a thing that Bessie would not have done for her big brother. What he wanted with so much money, she never asked.

They were still whispering together, and Clara had just risen to go upstairs. Alice and Will had finished the translation, and Will was just about to try throwing the *Commentaries of Caesar* into an ornamental Japanese jar across the room, when Mary opened the door and beckoned her children to come into the next room. Her face was pale, and she trembled as if with some great terror. The children all looked at each other in surprise and rushed into the next room.

2

THE DREAM

The Transformation Begins

ROBERT HARDY HAD FALLEN asleep on the couch by the open fire. In a short time—which in dreams can seem like a long time—he had a sort of vision. A profoundly vivid and disturbing vision.

It seemed to Robert that he stepped at once from the room where he lay into a place like he had never seen before, where the one great idea that filled his entire thought was that of the Present Moment. Spread out before him in clear detail was a moving panorama of the entire world. He saw into every home, every place of business, every shop and every farm, every place of industry, pleasure, and vice on the face of the globe. And he could hear humanity's conversations, catch its sobs of suffering, even the meaning of unspoken thoughts of the heart.

He fancied that over every city on the globe was placed a glass cover through which he could look and through which he could hear the thoughts of the inhabitants. He could envision all they were doing and suffering. He looked for the place of his own town, Barton. The first thing he saw was his minister's home. It was just after the Sunday evening service, the one Robert had thought so dull. Reverend Jones was talking over the evening with his wife.

"I feel so discouraged," he said. "What use is all our praying and longing for the Holy Spirit when our own church members are so apathetic and indifferent? You know I made a special plea to all the members to come out tonight, yet only a handful were there. I feel like giving up the struggle. You know I could make a better living in literary work, and the children could be better cared for then."

"But, John, it was a bad night to go out. The weather was awful. You must remember that."

"But only fifty people out of four hundred, most of them living nearby! It just doesn't seem right to me."

"Mr. Hardy was there," she said. "Did you see him?"

"Yes, after service I went and spoke to him, and he treated me very coldly. And yet he is the most wealthy, and in some ways the most gifted, church member we have. He could do great things for the good of this community, if only—"

Suddenly, in Robert's dream the minister changed into the Sunday school superintendent, who was walking down the street thinking about his responsibilities.

"It's too bad," he muttered to himself. "That class of boys I wanted Mr. Hardy to take on drifted away from church because no one could be found to teach them. And now Bob Wilson has got into trouble and been arrested for petty thieving. It will be a terrible blow to his poor mother. Oh, why is it that men like Mr. Hardy cannot be made to see the importance of work in Sunday school? With his knowledge of chemistry and geology, he could have reached that class of boys and invited them to his home and into his laboratory. He could've influenced them in great ways. I can't understand why men of such possibilities do not realize their power!"

The superintendent passed along, shaking his head sorrowfully. Robert, who seemed guided by some power he could not resist, and compelled to listen whether he liked it or not, found himself looking into one of the railroad-shop tenements. He saw Ward Scoville lying on a bed, awaiting amputation of both feet after the terrible accident. Scoville's wife sat on a ragged couch, while Natalie, the cook, knelt by her side. In her native Swedish tongue, she tried to comfort her poor sister.

Old Scoville was still conscious and suffering unspeakably. The railroad surgeon had been sent for, but had not arrived. Three or four men and their wives had come in to do what they could. Mr. Burns, the foreman, was among them. One of the men spoke in a whisper to him.

"Have you been to see Mr. Hardy?"

"Yes," Mr. Burns answered, "but he was at church. I left word about the accident."

"At church! So even the Devil sometimes goes

to church! What for, I wonder? Will he come here, do you think?"

"I couldn't say," replied Mr. Burns curtly.

"Do you remember when Scoville saved Mr. Hardy's life?"

"I remember it well enough," Burns said. "I was standing close by."

"What'll become of Scoville's children if he should pass away?"

"Don't know," Burns said solemnly.

Just then, the surgeon came in and began making preparations for the operation. The last that Robert heard was the shriek of his poor wife as she struggled to her feet and fainted, collapsing on the floor. Two of the youngest children clung terrified to her dress.

The father cried out, tears of agony and despair running down his face, "My God! What a hell this world is!"

In an instant, Robert's dream shifted to a different scene. He looked upon a room where everything appeared confused at first, but finally grew more distinct and terrible in its significance. The first person Robert recognized was his oldest son, George, in company with a group of young men who appeared to be engaged in … he couldn't tell at first. He rubbed his eyes and looked closely. Yes, they were gambling. So here was where George spent all his money, and Bessie's, too. Nothing that Robert had seen so far cut him as sharply as this.

The thought that his own son had fallen into this pit was terrible to him. But he was compelled to look and listen. All the young men were smoking and drinking plentifully.

"Hey, George," said a very flashily dressed young man who was smoking a cigarette, "your old man would rub his eyes to see you here, eh?"

"No doubt he would!" replied George, as he shuffled the cards and then helped himself to a drink.

"George," said the man, "your sister Bess is very good-looking. Introduce me, will you?"

"Not on your life!" snapped George. He seemed nervous and irritable.

"Oh, I'm not good enough for her, eh?" the fellow said.

George made a disparaging reply, and the other man punched him in the face. Instantly, George sprang to his feet, and fists began flying. Robert could not bear to watch any longer.

He closed his eyes and opened them to find himself looking into his own home. It was an evening when he and all the children had gone out and Mary sat alone, looking sadly into the fire. She was thinking, and her thoughts were like burning coals as they fell into Robert's heart and scorched him as no other scene, not even the last, had done.

"What has happened to my husband?" Mary murmured to herself. "How long has it been since he gave me a caress, kissed me when he went off to work, or laid his hand lovingly on my cheek as he used to do?"

She sobbed quietly and continued her sad musings. "How brave and handsome and good I used to think him in the old Vermont days when we were struggling for our little home! But the years have changed him. I wonder if he even realizes the distance between us. Does he realize I don't care about all the luxuries his money brings—and that all I really want is a loving, affectionate husband? Robert, can't you see that I'm so lonely? Can you be the person you once were?"

Mary fell on her knees by the side of the couch and buried her face in its cushions and sobbed and prayed.

Suddenly, the whole scene changed. Robert, who had stretched out his arms to comfort his wife as in the old days, felt himself carried by an irresistible power up away from the earth, past the stars and planets and suns. He traveled on and on, for what seemed to him like ages of time, until even the thought of time grew indistinct.

On and up he flew into the presence of the most mighty Face he had ever seen. It was the Face of Eternity. On its brow was written, in letters of blazing light, one word: "Now." And as he looked into that calm but fierce Face and read that word, Robert felt his soul sink within him. When the Face spoke, it was the speech of a thousand oceans heaved by a million tempests, yet through the terror of it ran a thread of music—a still, sweet sound.

And the Face said, "Child of humanity, you have neglected and despised me for fifty years. You have lived for yourself. You have been careless and thoughtless of the world's great needs. The time of your redemption is short. It has been appointed by Him who rules the world that you should have but seven more days to live on the earth, seven days to redeem your soul from everlasting shame and death. Mortal, see to it that you use this precious time wisely. I who speak to you am Eternity."

Then Robert Hardy fell prostrate before that Face and begged for a longer lease of life.

"Seven days! Why, it will be but seven swift seconds to redeem my past! Seven days. It will be a nothing in the marking of time. Grant me longer—seven weeks, seven years. And I will live for you as no mortal has yet lived."

Robert Hardy sobbed and held his arms up toward that most resplendent Face, which bent down toward his, and he thought a smile of pity gleamed on it, that perhaps more time would be granted him. Then, as the Face came nearer, Robert suddenly awoke to his own wife bending over him. A tear fell from her face on his own as she said, "Robert! Robert!"

Robert had sat up, confused and trembling. Then he'd clasped his wife to him and kissed her as he used to do. To her great amazement, he related to her in a low tone the dream he had just had.

Mary had listened in the most undisguised astonishment. But what followed filled her heart with fear.

"Mary," Robert said with the utmost gravity, "I cannot regard this as *just* a dream. I awoke with the firm conviction that I have only seven days left to live. I feel that God has spoken to me, and I have only seven days more to do my work in this world."

"Oh, Robert," she had tried to reassure him, "it was only a dream."

"No, it was more, Mary," Robert told her. "You know I am not superstitious in the least. This was something else. I will leave this world a week from tonight. Are the children here? Call them in."

Robert spoke in a tone of such calm conviction that Mary was filled with wonder and fear. That's when she had hurried from the room and called the children to come with her.

Robert gazed on his children with unfamiliar intensity. He related his experience, omitting any mention of the scene where George had appeared. Then he said, "My dear children, I have not lived as I should. I have not been to you the father I ought to have been. I have lived a very selfish, use-less life. I have only seven more days to live. God has spoken to me. I am—"

He broke off suddenly, sobbing, and drew his wife toward him and caressed her. Bess crept up and put her arms about her father's neck. The terrible thought shot into Mary's mind that her husband was insane, and Alice seemed to catch the reflection of her mother's fear. The other family members gave each other worrisome looks that implied their father might be delusional.

Robert interpreted these expressions and said, "I know what you're thinking. No, I am not sick or insane. I never was more calm and rational. But I have looked into the Face of Eternity tonight, and I know that in seven days God will require my soul." He turned to his wife with an anguished cry: "Mary, do you believe me?"

She peered into Robert's face and saw no hint of irrationality or madness. There was Robert's face now lighted up with the old love, exuding warmth and sympathy.

"Yes, Robert, I believe you," Mary said at last. "You may be mistaken in this impression about the time left for you to live, but you are not insane."

"Oh, Mary, I thank you for that!" he cried.

There was a pause. Then Robert asked George to bring the Bible. He read from the gospel of John and then prayed as he had never prayed before that, in the week allotted him to live, he might know how to bless the world and best serve his Master.

When Robert arose and looked at his wife and children, it was with the look of one who has been in the very presence of the living God. At the same moment, so fast had time gone in the excitement, the clock on the mantel struck the hour of midnight. The first of Robert Hardy's seven days had begun.

3.

MONDAY

The First Day

ೋ

WHEN ROBERT WOKE ON the morning of the first of the seven days left to live, he was about to get ready for his day's business, as usual, when the memory of his dream flashed before him. He remembered its grave message and wondered where he should begin, what he should do first.

Breakfast was generally a hurried and silent meal with him. The children came straggling down at irregular intervals, and it was very seldom that the family all sat down together. Mary was agitated and anxious, and yet the love and tenderness she felt from her husband gave her face a radiance that it had not shown for years.

The children were affected in various ways by their father's remarkable change. George was sullen and silent. Will looked thoughtful and troubled. Alice, a girl of strong opinions and character, greeted her father with a kiss and a look of understanding. Clara appeared terrified, as if death had already come into the house, and several times she broke down crying at the table. Bess sat next to her father, as she always did, and was the most cheerful of all, taking a very calm and philosophical view of the situation.

Robert was pale but composed. It would have been absurd to call him insane. He was naturally a man of strong will. Never in all his life had he felt so focused, so free from nervousness, so capable. The one great thought that filled his mind was of the shortness of time.

"Almighty God," was his prayer, "show me how to use these seven days in the wisest and best manner."

"Robert, what will you do today?" asked Mary.

"I have been thinking, dear, and I believe my first duty is to God. We have not had morning worship together for a long time. After we have knelt as a family in prayer to Him, I believe He will give me wisdom to know what I ought to do."

"I think Father ought to stay at home with us all the time," said Bess.

"Robert," said Mary, who still could not comprehend the full meaning of the situation, "will you give up your business? How can you continue while laboring under this impression?"

"I have already thought over that. Yes, I believe I ought to go right on. I don't see what would be gained by leaving the company."

"Will you tell the company you have only—" Mary could not say the words. They choked her.

"What would you do, Alice?" asked her father, turning to his oldest daughter, who had more than once revealed to the family great powers of judgment and decision.

"I would not say anything to the company about it," replied Alice finally.

"That is the way I feel," said Robert with a nod of approval. "They would not understand it. My successor in the office will be young Wellman, and he is perfectly competent to carry on the work. I feel as if this matter were one that belonged to the family."

Robert, who was a man of methodical business habits, had always arranged his affairs to plan for an accident. His business as manager required a great deal of travel, and he realized the liability of sudden death.

But such a thought had not influenced him to live less selfishly. He had thought, as most men do, that he should probably never need such preparations, that death might take the engineer or conductor or fireman, but would pass him by.

Suddenly, Will spoke up. "Father, do you want George and me to leave college?"

"Certainly not, my boy. What would be gained by that? I want you to keep right on just as if I were going to live fifty more years."

George did not say anything. He looked at his father as if he doubted his sanity. His father noticed the look, and a terrible wave of anguish swept over him as he recalled seeing his eldest son in the gambling room.

Again, the prayer he had been silently repeating all morning went up out of his heart: "Almighty God, show me how to use the seven days most wisely."

"Father," said Bess suddenly, "what will you do about Jim and Clara? Did you know they were engaged?"

"Bess!" said Clara passionately. Then she stopped suddenly, and, seeing her father's brow grow dark, she cowered, afraid of what was coming.

But Robert looked at the world differently this morning. Twenty-four hours before, he would have treated Bessie's remark as he usually treated her surprising revelations of the secrets of the family. He would have laughed at it a little and then sternly commanded Clara to break the engagement at once. James Caxton was not at all the sort of man Robert wanted to have come into his family. He was poor, to begin with. More than that, his father had been the means of defeating Robert in a municipal election where a place of influence and honor was in dispute. Robert had never forgotten or forgiven it. When he began to see his children becoming friends with the Caxtons, he forbade their going to the house.

Robert now looked at Clara and said tenderly, "Clara, we must have a good talk about this. You know your father loves you and wants you to be happy and—" Robert stopped, in his emotion, and Clara burst into tears and left the table.

"Come!" cried Robert after a moment, during which no one seemed inclined to speak. "Let us ask God to give us all wisdom at this time."

George made a motion as if to go out.

"My son," called Robert after him gently, "won't you stay with the rest of us?"

George sat down with a shamefaced look, and Robert asked God's help and blessing on all that day. He sat down for a moment by his wife and kissed her, putting his arm about her, while Bess climbed up on the side of the couch and the boys stood irresolute and wondering. Any outward mark of affection was so unusual on the part of their father that they felt awkward in the presence of it. Mary was almost overcome.

"Oh, Robert, I cannot bear it," she said. "Surely, it was nothing more than a dream. It couldn't have been anything more. You are not going to be called away from us so soon."

"Mary, I wish to God that I had seven years to atone for my neglect and selfishness toward you alone. But I am certain that God has granted me but seven days. I must act. God help me! Boys, you will be late. We will all be at home this evening. Alice, care for your mother and cheer her up. You are a good girl and—"

Again Robert broke down as he thought of the many years he had practically ignored his brave, strong, uncomplaining daughter. He was deeply saddened to remember how he had discouraged the poor girl's ambitious efforts to make her way as an artist. He looked at the girl now as she limped across the floor to her mother, her pale, intellectual face brightened by love and her eyes shining with tears at her father's unusual praise.

Oh, God, Robert prayed silently, *what have I done when I had it in my power to create so much happiness?*

The thought almost unnerved him; and for a moment he felt like sitting down to do nothing. But only for a moment. He rose briskly and said, "I am going down to see poor Scoville first thing. I shall be so busy, you must not look for me at lunch. But I will be back by dinner. Good-bye!"

He kissed his wife tenderly. Then he kissed his daughters, a thing he had not done since they were babies, shook hands with the boys, and marched out with deep heaviness, tears glistening in his own eyes.

Robert hurried down to the rough neighborhood where Ward Scoville lived, considering as he went along his plans for the man's future happiness and comfort.

"I'll pay the mortgage of his house free and clear," he said to himself. "It will be the best I can do for him. Poor fellow! What a shame I did not come down last night. And, as Mary said, his wife is an invalid and his oldest child only four years old."

He was surprised as he drew near the house to see a group of men standing outside and talking together earnestly. As Robert came up, they stood aside to let him pass, but were barely civil.

"Well, Stevens," Robert inquired of one of the men, recognizing him as one of the employees in the casting room, "how is Scoville this morning?"

"Dead," the man said immediately.

Robert reeled as if struck by a heavy blow.

"Dead, did you say?"

"He died about an hour ago," said one of the other men. "The surgeon was late in getting around and, after the amputation, we learned that Scoville had severe internal injuries."

"Was he conscious?" Robert asked the question mechanically, but all the while his mind was in a whirl of remorse.

"Yes, to the last moment."

Robert went up to the door and knocked. A woman, one of the neighbors, opened it and let him in. The sight stunned him. The dead man's body had been moved to a rear room, but his wife lay on the same ragged couch Robert had seen in his dream. The surgeon was bending over her. The room was full of neighbors.

The surgeon suddenly rose and, turning about, spoke in a quiet but decided tone: "Now then, good people, just go home, will you? And suppose some of you take these children along with you. You can't do anything more now, and your presence disturbs the woman. Ah, Robert!" he exclaimed. "You here? This is a sad business. Come, now, ladies, I must ask you to leave."

Everybody went out except the surgeon, the poor woman's sister, and Robert. He drew the surgeon over to the window and inquired concerning the particulars. Robert was visibly troubled, and he trembled violently.

"Well, you see," explained the surgeon, "Scoville was a dead man from the minute of the accident. Nothing could have saved him. When the accident happened, I was down at Bayville attending the men who were injured in the wreck last Saturday. I sent word that I would come at once. But there was a delay on the road, and I did not get here until three o'clock in the morning. In the meantime, everything had been done that was possible. But nothing could save the poor fellow. The shock of it all might just kill his wife. I wonder if she'll make it through the day."

"What will happen to the children?" Robert asked the question mechanically, again feeling the need of time to think out what was best to be done.

The surgeon shrugged his shoulders. He was accustomed to scenes of suffering and distress. "Orphans' home, I suppose," he replied laconically.

A movement and a moan from the woman called the doctor to her side. Robert, left alone, thought a moment. Then he stepped over to the surgeon and asked him if he could go into the other room and see the dead man. The surgeon nodded a surprised assent, and Robert stepped into the rear room and closed the door. He drew back the sheet from the face of the man and looked down on it. Nothing in all his experience had ever moved him so deeply. The features of the dead man were fixed in an expression of despair. Robert gazed steadily on it for half a minute, then, replacing the sheet, he knelt down by the side of the bed and prayed to God for mercy.

"Oh, Lord," he groaned in his remorse, "I plead with you not to hold me responsible for this man's death."

Yet, even as he prayed, he could not drive back the thought that chased across the prayer: "I am this man's murderer! I issued the order compelling the Sunday work. I refused a week ago to inspect the shop works that were declared unsafe, on the ground that it was not my business. I compelled this man to work under the fear of losing his job if he refused to do so. I, a Christian by profession, a member of the church, a man of means—I put this man in deadly peril in order that more money might be made and more human selfishness might be gratified. And this man once saved my life. I am his murderer—and no murderer shall inherit the kingdom of God."

Robert did not know just how long he knelt there in that bare room. At last he arose wearily and came out; his prayer had not refreshed him. The surgeon glanced at him inquisitively but asked no questions. Scoville's wife was in a state of shock. Natalie, the widow's sister and the

Hardys' cook, sat listlessly and worn out by the side of the couch. Just as the surgeon and Robert were going out together, the minister, Reverend Jones, appeared.

He looked surprised at seeing Robert, asked the doctor for details of the tragic death, and at once asked if he could see the poor Mrs. Scoville. The doctor thought it would do no harm.

Passing by, the pastor whispered to Robert, "She was a faithful member of our church, you know."

Robert did not know it, he confessed, to his shame. This sister of his in Christ had been a member of the same church and he had not even known it. If she had happened to sit on the same side of the sanctuary where he sat, he would probably have wondered who that plain-looking person was, dressed so poorly. But she had always sat back on the other side, being one of a few poor women who had been attracted into the church and comforted by Reverend Jones' simple piety and prayers.

The minister knelt and said a gentle word to the woman. Then he began a prayer of remarkable beauty and comfort. Robert wondered, as he

listened, that he could ever have thought this
man dull in the pulpit. He sat down and sobbed
as the prayer went on and consoled himself in it.
When Reverend Jones rose to leave, Robert rose
also and they went away together.

"Reverend," said Robert as they walked
along, "I have an explanation and a confession to
make. I haven't time to make it now, but I want
to say that I have met God face-to-face within
the past twenty-four hours, and I am conscious
for the first time in years of the intensely selfish
life I have lived. I need your prayers and help.
And I want to serve the church and do my duty
as I never before have done it. I have not supported your work as I should. I want you to think
of me this week as ready to help in anything
within my power. Will you accept my apology for
my contempt of your request a week ago? I will
come into the meeting Wednesday night and help
in any way possible."

Reverend Jones' eyes filled with tears. He
grasped Robert's hand and said simply: "Brother,
God bless you! Let me be of service to you in any
way I can."

Robert felt a little better for the partial confession.

He parted with his minister at the next corner as he turned down a street headed toward his office.

———◆———

It was now ten o'clock and the day seemed to him cruelly brief for the work he had to do. He entered the office, and almost the first thing he saw on his desk was the following letter, addressed to him but written in a disguised hand:

Mr. Hardy,

Us in the casting-room dont need no look-ing after, but maybe the next pot of hot iron that explodes will be for you if you thinks we have bodies but no souls some morning you will wake up believing another thing. We aint so easy led as sum supposes. Better look to house and employ speshul patrol; but if you do he will anser to us.

There was no signature to this threatening scrawl, which was purposely misspelled and poorly written. Robert had received threats before and paid little attention to them. Still, this morning he felt disturbed. His peculiar circumstances made the whole situation take on a more vivid coloring. Besides all that, he could not escape the conviction that he was responsible for the accident in the casting room. It was not his business to inspect machinery. But he was aware of it, and he felt now he had been criminally negligent in not making the inspection in the absence of the regular officer. An investigation of the accident would free Robert from legal responsibility, but in the sight of God he felt that he was morally guilty.

At that moment, Mr. Burns came in. He looked sullen and spoke in a low tone. "Only half the men are back this morning, sir. Scoville's death and the injuries of the others have had a bad effect on the workers."

Robert crumpled the letter nervously in his hand.

"Mr. Burns, I would like to apologize to you for my neglect of the injured men. Who are they and how badly are they hurt?"

Burns looked surprised, but gave a report, briefly describing the accident.

Robert listened intently with bowed head. At last he looked up and said abruptly, "Come into the casting room."

They went out of the office, passed through the repairing shops, and entered the foundry department. Even on that bright winter morning, with the air outside so clear and cool, the atmosphere in this place was murky and close. The forges in the blacksmith room at the far end glowed through the smoke and dust like smoldering piles of rubbish. Robert shuddered as he thought of standing in such an atmosphere all day to work at backbreaking toil. He recalled with a sharp vividness a request made only two months before for dust fans that had proved successful in other shops, and which would remove a large part of the heavy, coal-laden air, supplying fresh air in its place. The company had refused the request and had even said through one of its officers that when the men wore out, the company could easily get more.

Robert and the foreman paused at the entrance to the casting room, where the men had been injured the day before. A few were working sullenly. Robert asked the foreman to call the men together near the other end of the room; he wanted to say something to them. They dropped their tools and came over to where Robert was standing. They were mostly Scandinavians and Germans, with a sprinkling of Irish and

Americans. Robert looked at them thoughtfully. They were a hard-looking crowd.

Then he said very slowly and distinctly, "You may quit work until after Scoville's funeral. The machinery here needs overhauling."

The men stood impassive for a moment. Finally, a big Dane stepped up and said, "We be no minded to quit work these times. We no can afford it. Give us work in some other place."

Robert looked at him and replied quietly, "Your wages will go on while you are out."

There was a perceptible stir among the men. They looked confused and incredulous. Robert still looked at them thoughtfully.

Finally, the big Dane stepped forward again and said, speaking more respectfully than he did at first, "Mr. Hardy, we be thinking maybe you would like to help toward him the family of the dead and other as be hurt. I been 'pointed to take up purse for poor fellows injured. We all take hand in it. My brother be one—lost his two eyes."

A tear rolled down the grimy cheek of the big man and dropped into the coal dust at his feet. Robert realized that he was looking at a brother. He choked down a sob, and, putting his hand in his pocket, pulled out all the change he had and poured it into the Dane's hand. Then, seeing that it was only four or five dollars, he pulled out his wallet and emptied that of its bills. All the while, Burns and the men looked on in wonder.

"I'll do something more as well," Robert said.

He walked away feeling as if the ground were heaving under him. What was all his money compared with the life that had been sacrificed in his factory? He could not banish from his mind the picture of Scoville's face as it had looked to him when he drew back the sheet and gazed at it.

Robert hurried back to the office through the yard and sat down at the well-worn desk. The mail had come in and half a dozen letters lay there. He looked at them and shuddered. What did it all amount to, this grind of business, when the heartache of the world called for so much sympathy? Then he was overwhelmed by the sense of his obligations to his family: Clara's need of a father's guidance; George's need for help to leave bad influences; Alice's need of sympathy; his wife's need of affection and support; the church's need for involvement; the Scoville family's need to be provided for. On and on it went.

All these things crowded in on him, and still he saw the face and heard the voice of Eternity: "Seven days more to live!"

He sank into his thoughts for a moment. He was roused by the sounding of the noon whistle. Noon already? He turned to his desk, picked up his letters, glanced over them hurriedly, and gave directions for the answers of some of them to his impatient clerk, who had been wondering at his employer's strange behavior this morning. Among the letters was one which made his face burn with self-reproach. It was an invitation to a club dinner to be given that evening in honor of some visiting railroad president.

It was just such an occasion as he had enjoyed very many times before, and the recollection brought to mind the number of times he had gone away from his own home and left his wife sitting drearily by the fire. He tossed the invitation fiercely into the wastebasket and, rising, began pacing the room. He had so much to do and so little time to do it in! Then he went out and walked rapidly over to the hotel where he was in the habit of getting lunch when he did not go home. He ate a little and then hurried out.

As he was going out on the sidewalk, two young men came in and bumped into him. They were smoking and talking in loud voices, and Robert caught the sound of his own name. He looked at the speaker, and it was the face of the young man he had seen in his dream, the one who had insulted George and struck him afterward. For a moment, Robert was tempted to confront the youth and inquire into his son's habits.

No, he said to himself after a pause, *I will have a good talk with George himself. That will be best.*

He hurried back to the office and arranged some necessary work for his clerk, took a walk through the other office, then went to the telephone and called up the superintendent of the Sunday school, who was a bookkeeper for a clothing manufacturer. He felt an intense desire to arrange a meeting with him as soon as possible, but he learned that the superintendent had been called out of town by serious illness in his old home and would not be back until Saturday. Robert felt a disappointment more keen than the occasion seemed to warrant. He was conscious that the time was very brief.

He had fully made up his mind that, so far as he was able, he would redeem his selfish past and make a

week such as few men ever made. Scoville's death had
revealed to Robert his powerlessness in the face of certain possibilities. He now feared he had lost his chance
to confess his lack of service to the Sunday school.

He sat down to his desk and under that impulse
wrote a letter that expressed in part how he felt.
Then he jotted down the following items to be sent
to the proper authorities of the railroad:

> Item 1: The dust in the blacksmith shop and
> in the brass-polishing rooms is largely unnec-
> essary. The new fans and elevator ought to be
> provided in both departments. The cost
> would be but a small item to the company and
> would prolong the life and add to the comfort
> of the employees. Very important.

> Item 2: Effort should be made by all railroad
> corporations to lessen Sunday work in shops
> and on the rails. All perishable freight should
> be so handled as to call for the services of as
> few men on Sunday as possible, and excursion
> and passenger trains should be discontinued,
> except in cases of unavoidable necessity.

Item 3: The inspection of boilers, retorts, cast-ings, machinery of all kinds, should be made by thoroughly competent and responsible men, who shall answer for all unnecessary acci-dents by swift and severe punishment in case of loss of life or limb.

Item 4: In case of injury or death to employ-ees, if incurred through the neglect of the company to provide safety, it should provide financial relief for the families thus injured, or stricken by death, and, so far as possible, arrange for their future.

Item 5: Any railroad could, with profit to its employees, have on its staff of salaried men a corps of chaplains or preachers, whose busi-ness it would be to look after the spiritual and emotional needs of the employees.

It was now three o'clock. The short winter day was fast drawing to a close. The hum of the great engine in the machine shop was growing wearisome to the manager. He felt sick of its throbbing tremor and longed to escape from it. Ordinarily, he would have gone to the club room and had a game of chess with a member, or else he would have gone down and idled away an hour or two before supper at the art museum.

He was haunted by the thought of the other injured men. He could not rest till he had personally visited them. He went out and easily found where the men lived. Never before did the contrast between the dull, uninteresting row of shop tenements and his own elegant home rise up so sharply before him. In fact, he had never given it much thought before. Now as he looked forward to the end of the week, and knew that at its close he would be no richer, no better able to enjoy luxuries than the dead man lying in Scoville's home, he wondered vaguely how he could make use of what he had heaped together to make the daily lives of some of these poor men happier.

Robert found the man who had lost both eyes sitting up in bed. He was a big, powerful man like his brother, the large Dane, and it seemed a pitiful thing that he should be lying there like a baby when his muscles were as powerful as ever.

The brother was in the room with the injured

man, and he said to him, "Olaf, Mr. Hardy come to see you."

"Hardy? Hardy?" queried the man in a peevish tone. "What do I know him to be?"

"The manager. The one who donate so very much moneys to you."

"Ah!" the man said with an indescribable inflection. "He make me work on a Sunday! He is why I lose my eyes! A bad man, Svord! I will no have anything to do with him!"

The old man turned his face to the wall, and would not even so much as make a motion toward his visitor. His brother mumbled an apology.

Robert replied in a low tone, "Say nothing about it. I deserve all your brother says. But for a good reason, I wish Olaf would say he forgives me."

Robert came nearer the bed and spoke very earnestly and as if he had known the man intimately. "I did you a great wrong to order the work on Sunday, and in not doing my duty concerning the inspection of the machinery. I have come to say so, and to ask your forgiveness. I may never see you again. Will you say to me, 'Brother, I forgive you'?"

There was a moment of absolute silence on the part of the big fellow, then a large and brawny hand

was extended and the blind man said, "Yes, I forgive. We learned that in the old Bible at Svendorf."

Robert laid his hand in the other, and his lips
moved in a prayer of humble thanksgiving.

He went out after a few words with the family
and saw all the other injured men. By the time he
had finished these visits, it was dark, and he turned
eagerly toward home. He was exhausted from the
day's experience, feeling as if he had lived in a new
world, and at the same time wondering at how fast
the time had fled.

He sighed almost contentedly to himself as he
thought of the evening with his family and how he
would enjoy it after the disquiet of the day. Mary
was there to greet him, and Alice, Clara, and Bess
gathered around him as he took off his coat and
came into the beautiful room where a cheerful fire
was blazing. Will came downstairs as his father
walked in, and in the brief interval before dinner
was ready, Robert related the scenes of the day.

They were all shocked to hear of Scoville's
death, and Mary at once began to discuss some
plans for helping the family. Bess volunteered to
give up half her room to one of the children, and
Alice quietly outlined a plan that was businesslike

and feasible. In the midst of this discussion, dinner was announced and they all sat down.

"Where is George?" asked Robert. Ordinarily, he would have gone on with the meal without any reference to the boy, because he was so often absent from the table. Tonight, he felt an irresistible longing to have all his children with him.

"He said he was invited out to dinner with the Bramleys," Clara answered.

Robert received the announcement in silence. He felt the bitterness of such indifference on the part of his older son.

When he knows I have such a little while left, could he not be at home? Robert thought. Then in self-reproach, he immediately had another thought: *How much have I done for him these last ten years to win his love and protect him from evil?*

After supper, Robert sat down by his wife, and in the very act he blushed with shame at the thought that he could not recall when he had spent an evening like this. He looked into her face and asked gently, "Mary, what do you want me to do? Shall I read as we used to in the old days?"

"No, let's talk together," replied Mary, bravely holding back tears. "I don't know what this all means. I have been praying all day. Do you still believe as you did this morning?"

"Mary, I am if anything even more convinced that God has spoken to me. The impression has been deepening within me all day. When I looked into poor Scoville's face, the terrible nature of my past selfish life almost overwhelmed me."

There was silence for a moment. Then Robert grew more calm. He began to discuss what he would do the second day. He related more fully his meeting with the men in the shop and his visits to those injured. Then he drew Clara to him and asked about her troubles in such a tender, loving way that Clara's proud, passionate, willful nature broke down, and she sobbed out her story to him as she had to her mother the night before.

Clara clung to her father in loving surprise. She was bewildered, as were all the rest, by the strange event that had happened to her father. She had never felt his love like this before. Forgetting for a while the significance of his dream, she felt happy in his presence and in his affection for her.

The evening had sped by, and as it drew near to midnight again, Robert Hardy felt almost happy in the atmosphere of that home and the thought that he could still, for a little while, create joy for those who loved him. Suddenly, he spoke of his other son.

"I wish George would come in. Then our family circle would be complete. But it is bedtime for you, Bess, and all of us, for that matter."

It was just then that they heard steps on the front porch and soft voices outside. The bell rang. Robert rose to go to the door as Mary clung to him in fear.

"Don't open the door, Robert!" she said. "I'm afraid for you!"

"Why, Mary, don't be alarmed," he reassured.

Nevertheless, he was a little startled. The day had been a very trying one for him.

He went to the door, his wife and the children following him close behind. He threw it wide open, and there, supported by two of his companions, was his son George, too drunk to stand without assistance. One of the boys keeping George from falling down Robert recognized from the hotel lobby at lunchtime.

As for George, he leered into the faces of his father and mother with a drunken look that froze their souls with despair.

Mary uttered a wild cry, then ran forward and,

seizing her elder boy, almost dragged him into the house. Robert, recovering from his first shock, looked sternly at the boy's companions and then shut the door.

And so it was that the first of Robert Hardy's seven days came to an end. What had begun with acts of charity and recompense ended with heartache.

4.

TUESDAY

The Second Day

ৼ

ORNING CAME, AS IT comes to the condemned criminal and the pure-hearted child alike. After a brief and troubled rest, Robert woke to his second day, the memory of the previous night coming to him at first as an ugly dream, but afterward as a terrible reality.

His boy drunk! Unable to stand. Practically unconscious.

He could not make it seem possible. Yet there in

the next room he lay, sleeping off the effects of the night before. Robert fell on his knees and prayed for mercy, again repeating the words, "Almighty God, help me to use the remaining days in the wisest and best manner."

After a family council, in which all of them, on account of their troubles, were drawn nearer together than ever before, Robert outlined the day's work: First, he would go and see James Caxton and talk over the situation between him and Clara. Then he would go down to the office and take care of some necessary details of his business. If possible, he would come home for lunch. In the afternoon, he would attend poor Scoville's funeral, which had been arranged for two o'clock. Mary announced her intention to go also.

Then Robert thought he would have a visit with George and spend the evening at home, settling matters regarding his own death. With this agenda in mind, he went away, after an affectionate good-bye to his wife and children.

George slept heavily until the middle of the morning, and then awoke with a raging headache.

Bess, who had never seen anyone drunk before, had gone into the room several times during the morning to see if her brother was awake. When George was helped to bed the previous night by his father and mother, she did not understand his condition. She had always adored her big brother, and had no idea of his habits. When he did finally turn over and open his eyes, he saw the young girl standing by the bedside. He groaned as he recalled the night and his mother's look.

Bess said timidly, as she laid her hand on his forehead, "George, I'm so sorry for you. Don't you feel well?"

"I feel as if my head might split open," he stammered. "It aches as if someone were chopping wood inside of it."

"Why?" asked Bess innocently. "Did you eat something rotten at the Bramleys'?"

George looked at his little sister curiously. Then, under an impulse, he drew her nearer to him and said, "Bess, I have been bad. I was drunk last night! Drunk, do you understand? And I know I've broken Mother's heart—and Father's, too, I suppose."

Bess was shocked at the confession. She put out her hand again.

"Oh, no, George!" Then, with a feeling of revulsion, she drew back and said, "How could you do such a thing, with Father feeling as he does?"

Bess sat down crying on what she supposed was a cushion, but which was in fact George's new hat, accidentally covered with one end of a comforter which had slipped off the bed. She picked herself up and held out the hat.

"You're always wrecking my things!" George exclaimed angrily. But the next minute, he was sorry for snapping at her.

Bess retreated toward the door, quivering under the injustice of the charge. At the door, she stopped. She had something of Clara's hot temper, and once in a while she let even her adored brother George feel it.

"George Hardy, if you think more of your hat than you do of your sister, all right! You'll never borrow any more of my allowance! And if I do wreck your things, I don't come home drunk at night and break Mother's heart. That's what she's crying about this morning—that, and Father's strange ways. Oh, what a mess. Sometimes I hardly want to go on living." And twelve-year-old Bess broke down in sobs of sorrow.

George forgot his headache for a moment. "Come on, Bess, let's make up. Honest, now, I didn't mean it. I was bad to say what I did. I'll buy a dozen hats and let you sit on them for fun. Don't go away angry. I'm so miserable!"

He lay down and groaned, and Bess went to him immediately, her anger quickly subsiding.

"Oh, let me get something to make your headache go away," she said. "And I'll bring you up something nice to eat."

Just then, their mother came in and sat down on the bed. She laid her hand on George's head as his sister had done.

The boy moved uneasily. He saw the distress on his mother's face, but he said nothing to express regret for his shameful behavior.

"Bess, will you go and get George his breakfast?" asked Mary. She and her son sat in silence for a while, the space between them filled with heavy thoughts. Finally, Mary turned to her son and said, "George, do you love me?"

George had been expecting something different. He looked at his mother as the tears fell over her face, and all that was still good in him rose up in rebellion against the debased part. He seized his mother's hand and held it to his lips, kissed it reverently, and said in a low tone, "Mother, I am unworthy. If you knew—"

He stopped himself as if on the verge of confession.

His mother waited anxiously, and then asked, "Won't you tell me everything?"

"No, I can't!" he cried.

George shuddered, and at that moment Bess came in bearing a tray with toast and eggs and coffee. Mary left Bess to look after her brother and went out of the room almost abruptly. George looked ashamed and, after eating a little, told Bess to take the things away.

She looked grieved, and he said, "I can't help it. I'm not hungry. Besides, I don't deserve all this attention. Bess, is Father still acting as if his impression—or dream or whatever it was—is true?"

"Yes, he is," replied Bessie with much seriousness, "and he's been acting very different. Warmer and kinder. He kisses mother and all of us good-bye in the morning. I just don't believe he is right, uh, intellectually."

Now and then, Bess got hold of a big word and used it for all it would bear. At her use of the word *intellectually*, George laughed a little, but it was a laugh tinged with bitterness.

He lay down and appeared to be thinking, and after a while said aloud, "I wonder if he wouldn't let me have some money while he's feeling that way?"

"Who?" asked Bess. "Father?"

"Why not?" he snapped. "Go on—you better take those things downstairs!"

George spoke with his "headache tone," as Clara called it, and Bess without reply gathered up the tray and went out. George continued to figure out in his barely sober brain the possibility of conning more gambling money from his father.

———◆———

Robert had gone at once to his neighbors, the Caxtons, who lived only a block away. He had not been on speaking terms with the family for some time, and he dreaded the meeting, owing to all his ingrained pride and stubbornness. But two days had made a great change in him and, as he rang the bell, he prayed for wisdom and humility. James himself came to the door with his overcoat on and hat in hand, evidently just ready to go out. He was startled to see Robert.

"Hello, James," he said with as much cordiality as he could muster. "If you're going out, I won't ask to come in, then. I'll just walk with you a bit."

So James stepped outside, and the two walked along together.

There was an awkward pause for a minute, then Robert said, "James, is it true that you and Clara are engaged?"

"No, sir," the young man said immediately. "That is, not exactly engaged. We would like to be."

Robert smiled in spite of himself.

James added in a quickened tone, "We would like to be." Then he added, "With your consent, of course, sir."

Robert walked on thoughtfully and then glanced at the young man beside him. He was six feet tall, and as Bessie had said, not particularly handsome. But he had a good face, steady blue eyes, and a resolute air, as of one who was willing to work hard to get what he wanted. Robert could not help contrasting him with his own prematurely broken-down son

George, and he groaned inwardly as he thought of the foolish pride that would bar the doors of his family to a young man like James Caxton simply because he was poor and because his father had won in a contested election in which the two older men were candidates for the same office.

Then he said, glancing at the young man with a businesslike look, "Supposing you had my permission. What are your prospects for supporting my daughter? Frankly, she has always had everything she wanted. What could you give her?"

A light flashed into James' eyes, but he said simply, "I am in a position to make a good annual income—in fact, an above-average income—next spring. Besides which, I earn something extra with my pen at home."

Robert did not reply to this. He said, "Do you know what a willful, quick-tempered girl Clara is?"

"I have known her since we were children, Mr. Hardy," James said. "I feel as if I know her about as well as you do."

A look of consternation crossed Robert's face. "Perhaps you know her better than I do. I do not know my child as I should." His tone was not bitter but intensely sad.

The young man had, of course, been wondering about this talk with Robert and had observed a certain softness and openness he hadn't noticed before. He looked at Mr. Hardy now and noted his pale, almost haggard, face and his extremely thoughtful appearance.

"Mr. Hardy," said James frankly, "you seem to be troubled. I wish I could—"

Robert held up a hand. "Thank you, James, but no. You can't help me any in this except—" a faint smile crossed his lips "—except that you might solve this trouble between you and my daughter."

"There is no trouble between us, sir," replied James simply. "You know I love her and have loved her for a long time. I believe I am able to support her and make her happy. Won't you give your consent, sir? We are not children. We know our minds."

James spoke earnestly. He was beginning to hope that the stern, proud man who had so curtly dismissed him a little while before would relent and give his blessing.

Robert walked along in silence a little way. Then he said almost abruptly, "James, do you drink?"

"No, I don't," he replied.

"Do you gamble?" Robert asked.

James suddenly looked indignant. "You forget my mother, Mr. Hardy." The reply was almost stern.

In fact, the sad story was known throughout town: Mrs. Caxton's younger brother had been ruined by gambling. He had come to the house one night and, in a fit of anger because his sister would not give him money to carry on his speculations, had threatened her life. James had interceded and, at the risk of his own life, had probably saved his mother's. Mrs. Caxton had been so unnerved that her health had suffered from it seriously. All this had happened when James was growing out of boyhood and into adolescence. But not a day had passed that the young man did not see a sad result of that great gambling passion in his own mother's face and disposition. He loathed the thought of a vice so debasing that it ignored all family ties and would stop at nothing to satisfy the craving.

Robert knew the story and he exclaimed: "Forgive me, James, I did not think!" Then, after a pause, "Are you a Christian? I mean, do you have a faith in the revelation of God to men through Jesus Christ, and do you try to live according to His teachings, with a supreme love for God? Do you

live every day as if it might be the last you would
have to live?"

James started. Was Mr. Hardy putting him
through some kind of test—or was he feeling out of
sorts? He had never heard him talk like this before.
He could see, however, that some powerful change
had taken place in Mr. Hardy's usual demeanor.

James was like thousands of young men: temper-
ate, honest, industrious, free from vices, moral, but
without any decided and certain religious faith.

Am I a Christian? he asked himself, echoing Mr.
Hardy's question. No, he could not say he was. He
always tried to do the right thing and treat all people fairly. But he'd never considered himself a
Christian, though he had never said so to anyone.
He had, in fact, never been confronted with the
question before.

Finally, he replied to Robert, "To be perfectly
honest, sir, no, I don't think I am a Christian. I certainly try to live my life by Christian principles and
always be fair and honest, but I've never called
myself a Christian by the strictest definition. As for
living every day as if it were my last, I've never really
thought about it. Do you think that is possible, sir?"

Robert did not answer. He walked along

thoughtfully. In the course of the conversation, they had reached the corner where the young man would turn down a street heading toward his office. There, the two paused.

"I want to have another talk with you," Robert said. "Today is Tuesday. Shall we meet again tomorrow evening? I want to see your father, also, and—" He was about to say that he wanted to ask the elder Caxton's forgiveness, but for some reason he stopped without doing so.

James exclaimed eagerly as Robert turned to go, "Then there is some hope in the matter of my love for Clara."

Again, Robert did not answer, but he looked into the young man's face with a solemn gaze. Then he shook his hand and turned abruptly on his heel and walked rapidly down the street.

———◆———

Robert Hardy reached his office just in time to see Burns, the foreman, go out of a side door and cross the yard. The manager followed him and entered the machine shop in time to see him stop at a machine at the farthest end of the shop and speak to the man at work there. The man was a Norwegian by the name of Herman.

He was running a planer, a machine for trimming pieces of cold metal just arrived from the foundry. He was at work this morning on one of the eccentric bars of a locomotive, and it was of such a character that he could leave the machine for several minutes to do the work. Burns talked with this man for a while and then moved across the floor to another workman, a small-boned, nervous little fellow who was in charge of a boring machine which drove a steel drill through heavy plates of iron fastened into the frame.

Robert came up just as Burns turned away from this man, and touched him on the shoulder. The foreman started and turned about, surprised to see the manager.

"Well, Burns, how goes everything this morning?" asked Robert.

"The men here are grumbling because they don't have a holiday, same as the men in Scoville's department."

"But we can't shut down the whole business, can we?" asked Robert with a momentary touch of his old attitude. "The men are unreasonable."

"I'm afraid there is going to be trouble, sir. I can feel it in the air," replied Burns.

Robert made no reply in words, but looked about him. Within the blackened area of the great shop, about two hundred men were at work. The whirl of machinery was constant. The grind of steel on iron was blended with the rattle of chains and the rolling of the metal carriages in their tracks. In the midst of all the clashing of matter against matter, through the smoke and din and dust and revolution of the place, Robert was more than usually alive this morning to the human aspect of the case. His mind easily went back to the time when he himself stood at one of these planers and did just such work as that big Norwegian was doing, only the machines were vastly improved now.

Robert was not ashamed of having come along through the ranks of manual labor. In fact, he always spoke with pride of the work he used to do in that very shop, and he considered himself able to run any piece of machinery in the shops.

But he could not help envying these men this morning. *Why,* he thought, *probably every one of them has at least seven weeks to live, and most of them seven months or years!* He continued to think, *I would give all my wealth if I might change places with any one of these men, and know that I would probably have more than a week to live!*

Robert walked back to his office, leaving the foreman in a condition of wondering astonishment.

"Something wrong in his works, I guess!" muttered Burns.

Robert sat down to his desk and wrote an order, releasing all the men who desired to attend Scoville's funeral in the afternoon. He did not have it in his power to do more, and yet he felt that this was the least he could do under the circumstances. The more he thought of Scoville's death, the more he felt the cruel injustice of it. The injuries were clearly accidental, but they might have been avoided with proper care for human life. Robert Hardy was just beginning to understand the value of humanity.

He worked hard at the routine of his office until noon. But his mind, a good part of the time, was with the men in the shops. He could not escape the conviction that if a railroad company had the willingness to do so, it could make the surroundings of these men safer and happier without getting less efficient work or jeopardizing profits. He resolved to do whatever lay in his power to make the men feel that they were re-garded as something more than machines.

At lunchtime, Robert went home, where he found George milling about. When the two of them sat down at the kitchen table for lunch, George looked at his father with curiosity rather than with any feeling of shame for the scene of the night before. When lunch was over, Robert called his son into the study for a little talk before going down to the funeral.

"I do not need to tell you, George," began his father quietly, "that I feel the disgrace of your drunkenness last night very bitterly. But I did not call you in here to reproach you for your vices. I want to know what you intend to do."

George sat in silence, looking a bit confused.

Robert paused, then went on again. "I am per-fectly aware, George, that you regard my dream as a fantasy and think I am probably out of my mind. Isn't that true?" He looked George full in the face and waited for a reply.

The young man stammered, "Well ... I— I just don't understand."

"At the same time," his father went on, "I real-ize that nothing but a conviction of reality could produce the change in me that you and all the rest of the family must acknowledge has taken place. And you must confess that I am acting far more rationally than I did before my dream occurred. It is not natural for a father to neglect his own children, and I have done it. It is not rational that he should spend his time and money and strength on himself so as to grow intensely selfish, and I have done that. My boy, you may doubt me, but I am firmly convinced that I shall not be alive after next Sunday. I am trying to live as I ought to live under those conditions."

Robert let those words sink in for a minute, and then continued. "My son, I want you to do as you know you ought to do under the circumstances. When I am gone, your mother and the girls will look to you for advice and direction. You will probably have to leave college for a little while. But I want you to promise me that you will not touch another glass of liquor or place another bet as long as you live."

George laughed a little uneasily, and then lied outright: "I don't see the harm of a card game once in a while just for fun. I don't play for stakes as some fellows do."

"George," said his father, looking at him steadily, "you have not told the truth. You were gambling only a few nights ago. It is useless for you to deny it. That is where the very liberal allowance I have given you has been squandered."

George turned deadly pale and sat with bowed head, while his father went on almost sternly. "Consider your mother, George, whose heart almost broke when you came in last night. I don't ask you to consider me. I have not been to you what a father ought to be. But if you love your mother and sisters and have any self-respect left, you will leave drink and gambling alone after this. In the sight of God, remember what He made you for. You are young. You have all of life before you. I would gladly give all I possess to stand where you do today and live my life over again. I can't do it. The past is irrevocable. But one can always repent. George, believe me, your mother would rather see you in your coffin than see you come home again as you did last night. We love you."

Robert could say no more. He laid his hand on the boy's head as if he were a young lad again and said simply, "Don't disappoint God, my boy." With that, he went out, leaving his son sitting there almost overcome by his father's powerful appeal, but not yet ready to yield himself to the voice within that spoke even more powerfully.

It was one o'clock when Robert came downstairs, and, as he walked into the room where Mary and the girls were sitting, he happened to think of some business matters between himself and his only brother, who lived in the next town, twenty miles down the road. He spoke of the matter to Mary, and she suggested that Will go down on the three o'clock train with the papers Robert wanted to have his brother look over and come back on the six o'clock in time for dinner.

Clara asked if she could go too, and Bessie added her request, as she had not seen her aunt for some time. Robert saw no objection to their going, only he reminded them that he wanted them all back at six. Alice volunteered to spend time with George at home while all the rest were gone, and Robert and Mary departed for the funeral, Robert's thoughts still absorbed for the most part with his older boy. Clara had asked no questions concerning the discussion with James,

and her father simply stated that they would
have a good talk about it in the evening.

———————◆———————

The tenement was crowded and, despite the
wintry weather, large numbers of men and women
stood outside Scoville's place in the snow. Robert
had ordered his sleigh, and he and his wife had
gone down to the house in that, ready to take
someone to the cemetery.

The simple service was impressive to Robert.
Most of the neighbors present looked at him and
his well-dressed wife in sullen surprise. Mary
noticed the looks with a growing discomfort, but
Robert was too much absorbed in his thoughts
of what he had done and left undone in this fam
ily to be influenced by the attitude of those
around him.

Reverend Jones offered a prayer for the comfort of God to rest on the stricken family. He then
read a short passage from John's gospel appropri-
ate to the occasion and said a few simple words,
mostly addressed to the neighbors present. The
poor widow had been taken to a small room

upstairs, where she lay on a bed, cared for by her sister.

The minister had nearly concluded his remarks when he was interrupted by shouting in the room above. Then there was a rapid movement in the narrow hall, and, with a scream of frenzy, Mrs. Scoville rushed down the stairs and burst into the room where the dead body of her husband lay. She had escaped from her sister and, crazed with grief, flung herself over the coffin, moaning and crying.

Mary was first to move toward the stricken woman. She finally succeeded in drawing her away into the other room, and there held her, gasping for breath, now that the brief strength was spent.

She cried feebly, "Oh, God! Oh, God, help me! Don't keep me here in this world any longer!"

For a moment, it seemed more than Robert could bear. As soon as possible, he got up and went out and stood silently until the body was brought out and placed in the hearse.

That ride in the gray of the declining winter afternoon was a bitter experience for Robert Hardy. He roused himself at the grave as he heard the words, "Raise us from the death of sin unto the resurrection of righteousness," and something like a gleam of hope shot through his heart at the words. He drove back with more peace of soul than he had thought possible. By the time he had reached the shop tenements, it was growing dark.

As they entered the house, the telephone rang in the little office adjoining the hallway. Robert went in and answered the call. After a series of sharp exclamations and questions, he returned to the room where Mary sat. By the light of the open fire, she could see that he was very pale and agitated. His overcoat was lying on the couch where he had thrown it as he came in. He hastily put it on, saying to Mary, "There has been an accident on the six o'clock train between Baldwin and here, and Burns has telephoned me to come down. Don't be alarmed."

Mary started up. "Why, Will and Bess and Clara were coming home on that train!"

"Mary, let us hope for the best." Robert's voice trembled, but he tried to speak calmly and comfortingly.

"What did Mr. Burns say? Tell me all, Robert."

"He said that the train was derailed and a dozen people killed and as many injured. I don't know any more. I must go at once!"

Robert was almost overwhelmed, yet he asked himself how many accidents had occurred this last year on the road without his giving much thought to the suffering of those families afflicted. Now perhaps it had come to him. Bidding his wife pray and hope, he rushed out of the house and down to the station.

Robert mounted the engine just as it pulled out of the station and started its run of fifteen miles. The snow was falling in large, moist flakes. It was growing warmer and the snow would probably turn to rain before long. He gazed at the narrow band of light on the track ahead and leaned forward as if to help the engine go faster. He did not speak while the train rushed on through the night.

———◆———

As the engine drew near the scene of the wreck, Robert saw a great crowd standing about the track. Before the train came to a stop, he jumped from the cab and struggled forward. The accident had occurred on a bridge that spanned a small river near the town in which Robert's brother lived.

The engine, mail car, two day-coaches, and two

sleepers had crashed through the bridge and, falling a distance of fifty feet, had partly broken through the ice of the frozen stream. The two sleepers had caught fire, and there was absolutely no means to fight the flames. Robert saw men down on the ice throwing handfuls of snow on the blazing timbers in a frantic attempt to drive back or put out the flames. He fell, rather than ran, down the steep, slippery bank of the stream, and then the full horror of the situation burst on him.

The baggage car had fallen in such a way that the trunks rested upright on the ice. One day-coach lay on its side, but had broken completely in two, as if some giant hand had pulled it apart. The other day-coach had fallen on one end, and a third of it was underwater. The other end, resting partly against the broken car, stuck up in the air. Robert was conscious of all this as he heard the groans of the injured and the cries of those begging to be released from the timbers under which they had been caught. But his own children! Never had he loved them as now.

Robert rushed about the wreck searching for his children, a great fear clutching at his heart as he thought of their probable fate. Suddenly, the sweetest of all sounds—Bessie's dear voice—came to him. The next minute he had caught up the child as she ran to him and hugged her to him as he hadn't done in many years.

"Where are Will and Clara?" he cried.

"Oh, Father, they're here, and Will wasn't hurt much more than I was, but Clara has fainted, and she is lying down over here."

Bess dragged her father out across the ice to the edge of the bank, where a number of the victims had been laid on the cushions of the seats, some dead, some dying. There lay Clara, very white and still, with Will bending over her, himself bleeding from several wounds about the head and hands. But he was conscious and trying to revive his sister.

Robert knelt in the snow by his son's side. Upon seeing him there, Will sobbed excitedly, "Oh, she's dead!"

"No," replied Robert, "she's not."

Clara stirred, and her lips moved, but she did not open her eyes, and then her father noticed that a strange mark lay over her face.

Somehow Robert succeeded in carrying the girl to the top of the bank and left her there in the care of brave-hearted women. He went back to help rescue other victims, many who were trapped and groaning for help. Before the night was done, the number of dead climbed to more than seventy-five. The scene in town, when the survivors finally arrived there, seemed to Robert to be out of a dream, as a great crowd of anxious, ashen-faced people—James Caxton the first among them—surged through the station and over the track looking for loved ones. Sorrow visited too many homes in Barton that night.

So the second of Robert Hardy's seven days drew to a close.

5.

WEDNESDAY

The Third Day

꽃

OBERT WOKE ABOUT eight o'clock, rested, but felt sore from his exertions of the night. His first thought was of Clara. When he had gone to sleep, the girl seemed to be resting without pain, but that strange mark across her face made them all anxious. It was not a bruise, but it lay like a brand across her eyes, which had not opened since Robert found her lying by the frozen stream.

James had insisted on staying in the house to be of service. Mary felt grateful for his presence as she watched for returning consciousness from Clara, who still gave no further sign of awakening, although she breathed easily and seemed to be free from pain. Every doctor and surgeon in town had been summoned to the scene of the accident. But Robert felt so anxious for Clara as he came in and looked at her that he went downstairs and asked James if he would go and see if any of the doctors had returned.

"Yes, sir. I'll go at once. How is she now, Mr. Hardy?" the young man asked anxiously.

"I honestly don't know," replied Robert, laying his hand on James' shoulder. "There is something strange about it. Get a doctor, if you can."

Robert went upstairs again and, with Mary beside him, knelt and prayed. "Oh, Lord," he pleaded, "grant that this dear one of ours may be restored to us again. Spare us this anguish, not in return for our goodness but out of thy great compassion."

Will and Bess lay in the next room. Will was feverish and restless, Bess quite peaceful, as if nothing out of the ordinary had happened.

"Where is George?" Robert asked his wife as he rose from his prayer.

"I don't know," she answered. "He started down to the train a little while after you did. Haven't you seen him?"

"No, Mary. God grant he may not be—" He did not dare finish his thought aloud.

Mary guessed it, and together the two sat hand in hand, drawn near by their mutual trouble and by all the events of that strange week.

Mary said, as she drew her husband's face near to her, "Robert, do you still have that impression concerning your time left to live? Do you still think this week is to be the end?"

Mary had a vague hope that the shock of the accident might have destroyed the impression of the dream. But her hope was disappointed.

"My dear wife," replied Robert, "there is not the least doubt in my mind that my dream was a vision of what will happen. There is no question but that after Sunday, I shall not be with you. This is Wednesday. How the days have flown! Mary, I would go mad with the thought if I did not feel the necessity of making this week the best week of my life. Only, I don't know what is most important to do. If it had been seven months, or even seven weeks, I might have planned more wisely. This accident, so unexpected, has complicated the matter."

He talked calmly with Mary about what he would do that day, and he was still talking when James came in with a doctor. He was just from the scene of the accident and bore marks of a hard night's work. His first glance at Clara was hard and professional. But as he looked, he grew very grave, and an expression of surprise came over his weary face. He laid his hands on the girl's eyes and examined them, then raised her hand and dropped it on the bed again.

Turning to Robert and Mary, the doctor said gently, "You must prepare yourselves for a terrible fact resulting from the accident to your daughter. She has suffered a shock that will probably render her blind as long as she lives."

Robert and Mary listened, pale and troubled.

The doctor spoke again slowly. "There is another thing you ought to be prepared for. In rare cases like this, it happens sometimes that a loss of hearing accompanies the loss of sight. And with the loss of sight and hearing, it is possible the shock has deprived your daughter of the power of speech. I do not know yet whether this has happened, but you must be prepared."

"Oh, poor child," murmured Robert, while Mary sat down and buried her face in the blankets and sobbed.

The doctor, after further examination, said nothing more could be done at present. He gave directions for certain necessary treatment and departed after checking Will and Bess and prescribing medication for them.

Robert went downstairs and quietly told James all that the doctor had said. To a man living on the verge of eternity, as Robert was, there was no time for evasions or the postponing of bad news. James took the news more calmly than Robert thought he would. It was evident he did not realize all that was meant by it.

"Can you still love Clara under these conditions?" asked Robert, looking at James with a sympathy that the young man could not help sense.

"Yes, sir, more than ever," he replied. "After all, is she not more in need of it than ever?"

"True," said Robert, "but what can you do with a helpless creature like that?"

"God help us, sir! If she were my wife now

and were dependent on me, don't you think I could care for her more tenderly than anyone else in the world?"

Robert shook his head. "This is a hard blow to me, James. I don't know just what to say yet. But it is possible the poor girl may not have to suffer all that. Indeed, the doctor said he could not tell for certain that loss of hearing and speech would follow. If it does, I cannot see how Clara can retain her reason when she recovers from the shock. James, I believe you are a good fellow. I have not forgotten my own youth, and I will not stand between you and your love for Clara. I had hoped we might have a good talk about the matter. This accident has made it impossible for a time, at least, but I confide in you as an honest, true man. We must wait for events to take shape. Meanwhile, let us pray to God to give us wisdom and lead us into the way we need to go."

James Caxton listened to Robert with a feeling of astonishment. This was not the Robert Hardy he had known all his life, but a new man. For a moment, his own hopes and fears were lost in the thought of such a great change. In a tumult of feeling he went home, after begging Mary to send him word if Clara became worse or if there were any service he could render the family.

Robert went back upstairs where Mary sat by the side of the injured girl.

"Mary," he said, "I must go down to the shops. You know I left word with Wellman to do what he could in the office until I could get down, but this accident has made it imperative that I be there myself. There are details the men cannot attend to. I can't do any more here, and I must do what I can for the sufferers. God has been merciful to us. When I heard Bessie's voice in that awful place, it seemed to me God was taking pity on me for the burden I am carrying this week. If she had been killed, I believe I'd have gone mad. Pray for me, sweetheart."

With a kiss and embrace, Robert left the house, and even in all her sorrow, Mary felt a great wave of joy flow through her at the thought of this love come back to her. As she went to the window and watched the tall, strong figure walk down the street, she felt like a girl again and wondered if he would turn around and tip his hat as he used to do.

Just before he reached the corner where he had to turn, he looked back up at the window, saw his

wife standing there, and took off his hat with a
smile. She felt the glow of love, as she had when
they courted years ago.

———————◆———————

Robert found much to do at the shops. It looked
to him as if he must be down there all day. Along
toward noon, Burns came into the office. He asked
Robert to step across the yard and talk to the men,
who, Burns said, had threatened to cause trouble if
they were not given the afternoon to go down to
the scene of the disaster. Robert rose with a sinking
heart and followed Burns into the planing rooms.
He told the foreman to get the men together in the
center of the room. They stopped their machines
and gathered in the largest open space between the
planers, and Robert addressed them.

"What do you want, men?" he said. "Burns tells
me there is dissatisfaction. Speak out so we may
know what the trouble is."

There was an awkward pause. Then one man
spoke up: "We think the company ought to give us
the day off."

"What for?" asked Robert mildly.

Under any other circumstances, he would have told the men they might leave for good if they didn't like the pay and the company. He had done just that thing twice before. But things were different now. He looked at the men in a new light. Besides, it was imperative that the work in the shops go on. The company could ill afford to lose the work just at this particular time. All these considerations did not blind Robert to his obligations as an officer of the company. He was only anxious that no injustice should be done.

Another man spoke up. "Our friends was in the accident. We want to go and see them."

"Very well," Robert replied. "How many men had relatives or friends in the accident who were injured or killed? Let them step forward."

For a moment, none of the men moved. Then three men stepped out.

Robert said, "You may go if you want to. Why didn't you ask for leave if you wanted it? Why would you suppose the company would refuse such a request? Now, what is the trouble with the rest? The company is not in a position to grant a holiday at this particular time and you know it. I can't shut down the shops all day to let you go and see a railroad wreck. Be reasonable. What do you want?"

"We want more pay and freedom from Sunday work," said the Norwegian who ran the biggest planer in the shop.

Robert replied, still speaking pleasantly: "The matter of more pay is one we cannot well discuss here now, but I will say to you that, as far as it is in my power, there shall be no more Sunday work demanded."

"Still, that is not the question," said the man in an insolent tone. Robert looked at him more closely and saw that he had been drinking.

Another man shouted, "Shut up, Herman! Mr. Hardy be right. We be fools to make trouble now."

A dozen men started for their machines to go to work again, while Burns went up and laid his hand on the Norwegian's arm and said to him roughly, "Quit now! You've been dipping that beard of yours into a whiskey barrel! Better mind yourself, or you get your walking papers!"

"Mind your own business, Burns!" replied the big man heavily. "You be somethings of a beard drinker yourself—if you had the beard!"

Burns was so enraged at the drunken retort that he drew back as if to strike the man, when the

Norwegian gave the foreman a blow that laid him sprawling in the iron dust.

Instantly, Robert stepped up between the two men before Burns could rise. He looked the drunken man in the face and said sternly, "You are discharged! I can't afford to employ drunken men in these shops. Leave this instant!"

The man leered at Robert and raised his arm as if to strike, but before the Norwegian could do any harm, two or three of the men seized him and hustled him back to the other end of the shops. A moment later, Burns rose, vowing vengeance.

The men went back to their machines and Robert, with an anxious heart, went back into the office, satisfied that there would be no trouble in the shops for the rest of the day at least. He was sorry that he had to fire Herman, but he felt that he had done the right thing. The company could not afford to employ men who were drunkards, especially at this time, when it began to be hinted that the result of the accident on the road was due to the intoxication of a track inspector.

That accident was a complication in Robert's seven days. It was demanding of him precious time that he longed to spend with his family.

Once that afternoon, as he worked at the office, he was tempted to resign his position and go home, come what might. But to his credit, be it said that always, even in his most selfish moments, he had been faithful to his duties at the office. At present, no one could fully take his place. So he stayed and worked on, praying as he worked for his dear ones, and hoping that Clara was better. He had been to the telephone several times and had two or three short talks with his wife; and now, just as the lights were turned on in the office, the bell rang again, and Mary told him that Reverend Jones had called and wanted to see him about some of the families that were injured in the accident at the foundry room.

"Tell Reverend Jones I will try to see him at the meeting tonight," he said. "And tell him I will have something to give him that he wants. How is Clara now?"

"No change yet," Mary answered. "Will is shaky and anxious. He says he had a horrible dream about the accident this afternoon. Bess is about the same. Her escape was a miracle."

"Has George come home yet?" Robert inquired.

"No," she replied. "I'm getting nervous about

him. I wish you would ask about him at the Bramleys' when you come home for dinner."

"I will," he assured her. "This has been a terrible day down here. God keep us. Good-bye."

Robert finished most of the work and started for home at six. On the way he asked around about George, but nobody had seen him since the previous evening. When he reached the house, he found that Mary, utterly worn out, had lain down and fallen asleep. Clara's condition had not changed. Alice reported that once in the afternoon she had moved her lips and distinctly called for water. Robert and Bess sat down to the supper table by themselves, and Bess again told how she had been saved from even a scratch in that terrible fall. It was indeed remarkable that the child did not suffer even from the general shock and reaction of the disaster.

As the evening wore on, Robert felt that his duty lay in his own home for that night, and he would have to see his minister some other time. Sitting by the bed of his unconscious daughter, he thought of the prayer meeting with regret, wondering how he could've been so indifferent toward opportunities for spiritual growth for so many years. He thought, *What irony that I now long to attend the church service but know I must be with my family during this time of grave need.*

———————◆———————

At the church, James Caxton opened the sanctuary door and handed a note to someone in the back pew, with the request that it be sent up to Reverend Jones. He then turned as if to go out, but hesitated, came back, and slipped into a vacant seat.

The minister received the note, quickly scanned its contents, and then rose. There was strong emotion in his voice as he spoke.

"I have just been handed a note from one of our members, Mr. Robert Hardy, with the request that I read it aloud to the church tonight." He then proceeded to read:

> To you, my dear pastor, and you, my brothers and sisters in Christ: I suppose it is known to most of you that three of my children were on the train during the recent accident, and two of them escaped with but slight injuries. But my daughter Clara was seriously injured by the

shock, and I am at this moment seated by her side, praying that her reason may be spared and her possible injuries prove to be curable. I had planned to be with you tonight. I wanted to tell the church of the change that I have lately experienced. I do not need to tell you that for the twenty-five years I have been a member of the church, I have been a member only in name. I have seldom participated in any of the spiritual or devotional services of the church. I have often been critical and judgmental. I have been cold and even vengeful toward other members of this church. I have been a proud, unchristian, selfish man. In the sight of God, I have been an unworthy member of the church of Christ. I do not take any pride to myself in making this confession, but I feel that it is due you, and something tells me I shall have more peace of mind if I speak to you as I have lately prayed to God.

It is not necessary to tell you how I have been brought to see my selfishness in all its enormity. It is enough if I say to you that I most sincerely believe I have misunderstood the right meaning of human existence. Let me say this also, as this may be my last opportunity to say to you what lies in my heart: Serve the church of Christ with enthusiasm and devotion, all you who have made a genuine commitment to it. Be loyal and loving toward one another—and most of all, toward God. I ask your prayers for me as your petitions go up for the afflicted and repentant everywhere.

Your brother in Christ,
    Robert Hardy

The stillness that followed the reading was deep and profound. After a moment, one of the oldest men in the room rose. With obvious conviction and sincerity, he prayed for Robert and thanked God for his guiding strength. The prayer was followed by others. Then a few of the members, who had not been on good terms with Robert, stood and confessed their spitefulness and asked forgiveness. As the meeting drew to a close, Reverend Jones asked if there were any present who wanted to begin the Christian life of which Robert spoke.

"I'm sure there are some here who don't know

Christ, who haven't put their trust in Him," the minister said. "Are there any who would like to say that they want to become Christians and will try to live the life of Christ every day?"

In the pause that followed, James Caxton felt as if some power within and without were lifting him to his feet. He grasped his chair as if to hold himself down. A battle raged within him: remain seated and silent, or stand and declare his desire to know Christ? He heard, more with his heart than with his ears, a voice that said, "Son, a new life awaits you, one that will be far more meaningful and satisfying than you've ever experienced before."

So James Caxton stood and said he wanted to be a Christian. Though he hardly knew what he was doing, that one small action brought a profound sense of peace and serenity to him.

———————◆———————

At the Hardy household, Robert kept vigil, watching and praying for his children. Will slept irregularly, being troubled with his dreams of the accident. Mary awoke and begged her husband to lie down and get a little rest. He did so, but was roused about ten o'clock by the doctor coming in. He had just finished a visit nearby; he saw the light and was anxious to see Clara. He examined her face very keenly, and then sat down by the bed for an instant. After giving certain medicines, he found that he was in need of another instrument, which was at his house.

"I will go and get it, Doctor," Robert said. "It's not far, and I think a little fresh air will do me good and help me to remain awake."

He went downstairs, and the doctor followed him as he went out into the hall and pulled on his overcoat. Robert turned before he opened the door.

"Doctor, tell me the truth about my girl," he said. "What is her condition?"

"It is serious, but more than that I cannot say," the doctor answered. "It is possible I have been wrong in my diagnosis. No one can say with certainty."

So Robert went out into the night with a glimmer of hope. It was snowing again and a strong wind was blowing, so he buttoned up his big coat and walked as rapidly as he could in the direction of the doctor's house. The streets were almost deserted. The lights at the corners flickered and showed pale through the lamps.

As he turned down a narrow street, intending to take a shortcut across a park that lay near the doctor's residence, he was suddenly surrounded by five young men.

"Give us your money!" one of them demanded in a drunken voice. "You've got plenty and we haven't. So hand it over or you'll be asking for trouble."

The young men crowded in closer around Robert.

He had been taken completely by surprise. His first impulse was to shake himself loose and make a run for it. His next glance, however, showed him these were not professional robbers, but young men about town who had been drinking late and were holding him up just for fun. What could he do? He knew two of them, the sons of the Bramleys, who were well-to-do people in Barton. The three other young men were in shadow, and he could not recognize them.

Robert's next thought was to insist they quit such a dangerous stunt and go on home. All this passed through his thoughts with a flash. But before he had time to do anything, a police officer sprang out of a doorway nearby, and the young men fled in different directions. The officer chased down one of the boys and dragged him back to where Robert stood.

"Here's one of the thieves!" the officer exclaimed. "We've been looking for this gang for some time now. Just a few nights ago, they robbed a man and his wife at the other end of the park. We figured they might be back, since this is an easy spot to surprise unsuspecting folks out for a stroll. Sir, identify this one, if you will. Tell me if he is one of the men who grabbed you."

The policeman dragged the lad under the light of the lamp and roughly took off his hat.

Robert looked into the young man's face and cried out, "George! Is it you?"

"Father!"

The two looked at each other in silence, while the snow fell in whirling flakes about them. Robert looked at his son in shock and dismay, at a loss for what to do or say. He had never been an affectionate father to his boys. He had generally given them money when they asked for it, without question about its use, but he had never been a companion to his sons.

In that moment, he was gripped by the realization that he'd provided little moral guidance and role modeling for George. Robert was seized by the sudden regret of knowing his son had gone wildly astray and he was at least partially to blame. Still, it didn't occur to him that the boy was guilty of a crime which might put him behind prison bars. His only desire was to get back home and have a thorough talk with him.

The police officer stared in wonder, but he did not relax his hold on George. He took an extra twist in his captive's coat collar and looked sharply at Robert, as if to say, "He may be your son, but he's my prisoner, and I mean to keep a good grip on him."

Finally, George spoke up. "Father, you know I wouldn't really do such a thing. We were only out for a little fun. We didn't know it was you, of course. We didn't mean any real harm. It was just a foolish prank."

"Foolish is right!" Robert nearly shouted. "And dangerous."

George said no more. Robert bowed his head and seemed to be thinking.

The officer, who had been waiting for another

move on the part of the older man, said, "Well, we must be moving on. It's warmer in the lock-up than out here. So come along and do your talking tomorrow morning with the rest of the drunks and delinquents."

"Wait!" cried Robert. "This is my son! Do you understand? What are you going to do?"

"Do?" the officer said immediately. "I'm going to book him for assault with intent to commit robbery."

"But you heard him say it was all a joke." Robert knew it sounded pathetic the moment he'd said it.

"A pretty joke to try to hold up a man and demand his money," the policeman retorted. "That doesn't sound like a joke to me. Sorry, but I'm bound to obey orders. Like I said, we've been after this gang of petty thieves for a month now."

"But you don't understand," Robert protested. "This is my son!"

The officer sneered at George. "Well, what of it? We send sons to the lock-up every day for some mischief or other. Do you suppose you are the only father whose son is getting into trouble?"

"But this is my boy!" Robert cried. "It would kill his mother to have him arrested and put in jail for trying to rob his own father."

"I'm sorry, sir," the officer said. "This boy must learn his lesson or he'll be right back in this park next week trying to rob someone else." He clutched George's coat a little harder and growled, "C'mon, kid. Maybe a night in jail will knock some sense into your thick skull."

And thus ended Robert Hardy's third day, with the sight of his oldest son being dragged off to jail.

6.

THURSDAY

The Fourth Day

**FTER AN ANXIOUS AND** restless night, which afforded Robert little sleep, he trudged first thing in the morning to the jailhouse. He wanted to check on his son and see if he had better luck convincing a different officer to release the young man.

There, Robert, looking wan and slightly disheveled, met the desk sergeant, a stout man named Gibson. Robert recognized the officer from an incident at the railroad shops a year earlier, in which a melee had broken out among several of the men. Sergeant Gibson and several other policemen had been called to restore order.

Robert explained the situation from the previous night, while the sergeant nodded and scratched his chin thoughtfully. Robert pleaded his case, arguing that there was no way he would press charges or testify against his own son.

The officer hesitated. Robert stepped nearer his son.

After a minute of deliberation, the sergeant said, "All right, Mr. Hardy. I'll authorize his release." He gave Robert a wry grin. "I know what it's like to have a son who gets into trouble. My own boy has had scrapes with the law. Can you believe that—the son of a police sergeant? How we fathers must worry and watch over them every moment!"

"I'm grateful for your understanding, Sergeant," Robert said.

"But let me warn you," Sergeant Gibson quickly added. "Next time—if there is a next time—there will be no leniency. Understood?" He paused. "Ah, but let us hope a night in jail has given the boy a taste of what life behind bars is really like."

———————◆———————

An hour later, Robert and George walked out of the jailhouse and toward home. George looked rumpled and weary—but also relieved to be free.

Suddenly, a thought occurred to Robert. "I'm not sure you've heard about the train accident."

"Yes, I heard some people talking about it," George replied. "Many killed and injured, they said. Sounds awful."

Robert stopped and put his hand on George's shoulder. "But what you probably don't know is that Will, Clara, and Bess were on that train."

George looked shocked. "No, Father! Were they hurt? Was Bess—" The boy seemed moved as his father had not seen him in a long time.

"Bess was not hurt at all," Robert explained. "But Will was severely bruised, and Clara still lies in a state of unconsciousness. We don't know what will happen to her. Last night, I was going to retrieve supplies from the doctor's house—that's why I was walking through the park."

They continued their trek toward home in silence.

When they at last came through the front door of the house, Mary came running downstairs. When George turned and faced her, she held out her arms, crying, "We have been so anxious about you!"

George wiped away a tear. Then, going up to his mother, he laid his cheek against hers, while she folded her arms about him. After a moment's silence, he stammered out a few words of sorrow at having caused her pain. And she listened to his explanation of how he had not known Clara and the others were involved in the train accident. It was true that he had gone out the evening before fully intending to go down to the scene of the accident. As he felt his mother's arms around him, and realized what the family had been enduring, he felt shame and disgrace.

Robert went upstairs to check on Clara. She did not seem to be in any great pain, but she was unconscious of everything around her.

After a short talk with his mother, George came up and inquired about Bess and Will. They were both sleeping, and the doctor had assured Robert and Mary the previous night that they would be fine.

George joined his parents in the room where Clara lay. Robert had said no more to George about the incident at the park and its aftermath. He was still shaken and filled with shame over his son's actions. But now, as the three sat silently together, Robert and Mary noticed their son had his hands folded, his head bowed, and his eyes closed. His face wore an earnest expression. His parents looked at each other curiously.

Could he be praying? Robert thought. It had been a very long time since he'd seen his son pray.

———◆———

As the morning progressed, the sky filled with snow, which whirled in wreaths around the sorrowing homes of Barton. Robert Hardy thought of the merciful covering it would make for the piles of ruin down under the bridge and along the banks of the river. He said to himself, "This is my fourth day. How can I best spend it? What shall I do?"

The morning went rapidly by and, before he knew it, noon was near. The time had passed in watching Clara, visiting with Bess and Will, and doing some necessary work for the company in his little office downstairs. He did not feel like talking further with George yet. James Caxton had visited, and the first thing he mentioned was his decision in the church meeting the night before. Robert thanked God for it, and a prayer went from his heart for his own son, that the Spirit might touch him and bring him into the light of Christ.

A little after noon, the storm cleared up and Robert prepared to go to the shops. Clara had not yet come out of her stupor. The doctor came to visit and found no change in the girl's condition. There was nothing in particular that Robert could do so he went out about one o'clock and entered his office, hoping that he would have no trouble with the men.

Mr. Burns reported everything quiet, and the manager, with a sigh of relief, proceeded with the routine duties of the business. As the uneventful afternoon went on, the storm ceased entirely and the sun came out clear and warm.

Toward three o'clock, one of Robert's old friends came in and said there was a general move-ment throughout Barton to hold a large mass meeting in the town hall for the benefit of the sufferers, both in the railroad accident and in the explosion of the Sunday before in the shops. It was true the company would settle for damages, but in many cases the payments would be slow in arriving.

"Can you come out to the meeting, Robert?" asked his friend.

He thought for a moment and replied, "Yes, I think I can." Already an idea had taken shape in his mind that he felt was inspired by God.

"It might be a good thing if you could come prepared to make some remarks," the friend told him. "I think the public is ready to charge the railroad with carelessness and mismanagement."

"I'll say a word or two," replied Robert.

Later, Robert spoke to his wife about the meeting, fearing that by agreeing to go he was using precious time that rightly belonged to his family.

"Robert," replied Mary, smiling at him through happy tears, "it is the will of God. Do your duty as He makes it clear to you."

"Father, what do you want me to do?" George asked. "Should I stay here?" He had not been out of the house all day.

Robert hesitated a moment, then said, "No, George, I would like to have you go with me. Alice can do all that is necessary here."

When Robert and George reached the town hall, they found a large crowd gathering. Robert went up to the platform, where the leader of the meeting greeted him and said he would expect him to make some remarks during the evening. Robert sat down at one end of the platform and watched the hall fill with people, nearly all well known to him.

Soon, the leader announced, "Mr. Robert Hardy, our well-known railroad manager, will now address us."

There was a murmur of curiosity and surprise from the audience, as many wondered what the wealthy railroad man would have to say on such an occasion.

Robert began in a low, clear tone. "Men and women of Barton, tonight I am not the man you have known these twenty-five years that I have been among you. As I stand here, I have no greater desire in my heart than to say what may prove to be a blessing to all my old townspeople and to my employees and to these strong young people. Within a few short days, God has shown me the selfishness of a human being's heart. That heart was my own, and it is with feelings none of you can ever know that I look into your faces and say these words."

Robert paused a moment as if gathering himself up for the effort that followed. The audience was hushed and expectant as this once proud and cold man lifted his arms and spoke with passion and conviction.

"There is but one supreme law in this world, and it is this: Love God and your neighbor with heart, mind, soul, strength. There are but two things worth living for: the glory of God and the salvation of man. Tonight, I feel the bitterness that comes from knowing I have broken that law and have not lived for those things that alone are worth living for."

He paused again, noticing how stunned the people looked. "People of Barton, why is it that we are so moved, so stirred, so shocked by death, when the far more important domain of life does not disturb us in the least? We shudder with terror in the face of death, we lose our accustomed pride or indifference, we speak in whispers and we tread softly, but in the presence of the living God we go our ways careless, indifferent, cold, passionless, selfish.

"I know what I am talking about," he continued. "I have lived like that myself. But death can't be compared for one moment with life for majesty, for meaning, and for power. There were seventy-five people killed in the accident. But in the papers this morning I read in the next column in small type and in the briefest of paragraphs, the statement that a young man in our town has been arrested for forging his father's name on a check."

Robert saw heads nodding, as if many had noticed the same thing in the newspaper.

"Such things occur every day in this town and all over the world," he said. "As we mourn the loss of friends, neighbors, and family members lost in the tragic accident, do we give a moment's thoughts to the spiritual and moral demise among many still living in our midst? How many mass meetings have been held in this town within the last twenty-five years over the loss of character, the death of purity, the destruction of honesty? Yet they have far outnumbered the victims of the latest disaster."

There was general stirring among the crowd. Robert realized he was sounding very much like a preacher—and he knew his words were probably inspiring to some and irritating to others. But he was not concerned if he bothered some people. His time was short, he believed, and he must say what was on his heart.

"And what does mere death do?" he continued. "It releases the spirit from its house on earth. Aside from that, death does nothing to the person. But what does life do? Life does everything. It prepares for heaven or for hell. It starts impulses, molds character, fixes destiny. Death is only the last enemy of the many enemies that life knows. Death is a second; life is an eternity.

"The greatest enemy of man is selfishness. This disaster, which has filled the town with sorrow, was due to selfishness. It has been proved by investigation already made that the accident was caused by a drunk track inspector. What was the cause of that drunkenness? The drinking habits of that inspector. How did he acquire them? In a saloon that we taxpayers allow to run on payment of a certain sum of money into our town treasury. So, then, it was the greed or selfishness of the men of this town which lies at the bottom of this dreadful disaster. Who was to blame for the disaster? The track inspector? No. The saloon keeper who sold him the liquor? No. Who, then? We ourselves, we who licensed the selling of the stuff. If I had stumbled over the three corpses of my own children night before last, I could have exclaimed in justice before the face of

God, 'I have murdered my own children,' for I was one of the men of Barton to vote for the license that made possible the drunkenness of the man in whose care were placed hundreds of lives."

He looked out among the sea of faces and spotted, toward the back, his son. George had a solemn and sorrowful expression on his face. Robert thought for a moment and then continued with his speech.

"What is it that you merchants and businessmen here tonight struggle with most? The one great aim of your lives is to buy for as little as possible and sell for as much as possible. What care have you for the poor who work at worse-than-starvation wages, so long as you can buy cheap and sell at large profits? To whom am I speaking? To myself.

"In order that the people may know that I am sincere in all I have said, I have set up a trust fund at the bank to be used for the education of children in bereaved homes or for any other help to those who need it. This money is God's. I have robbed Him and my brothers of it all these years."

Although the audience sat in rapt attention, Robert knew he must draw his comments to a close. So with all his passion and conviction, he made his last point.

"But the great question for us all is not this particular disaster. That will in time take its place as one event out of thousands in the daily life of this world. The great event of existence is not death, it is life. The great question of the whole world is selfishness in the heart of man. The great command is, 'Seek first the kingdom of God.' If we had done that in this town, I believe such a physical disaster as the one we lament would never have happened. That is our great need. If we go home from this meeting resolved to rebuke our selfishness in whatever form it is displeasing to God, and if we begin tomorrow to act out that resolution in word and deed, we shall revolutionize this town in its business, its politics, its churches, its schools, its homes. God help us all to do our duty! Time is short, eternity is long. Death is nothing, life is everything."

Years after this speech of Robert Hardy, one who was present in the audience described the sensation that passed through it when the speaker sat down to be like a distinct electric shock that flowed from seat to seat and held the people fixed and breathless. The effect on the leader of the meeting was the same. He sat motionless. Then a wave of emotion gradually stirred the audience and, without a word of dismissal, they poured out of the building and scattered to their homes.

Robert found George waiting for him at the back of the hall. The father was almost faint with the reaction from his address. George gave his arm and the two walked home in silence. Thus ended Robert Hardy's fourth day.

7.

FRIDAY

The Fifth Day

❧

THE WHOLE TOWN WAS talking about Robert Hardy's surprising address. Some thought he was crazy. Others regarded him as sincere. But after the first effect of his speech had worn off, many criticized him severely for presuming to "moralize" on such an occasion. Still others were bewildered, unable to account for the change in the man.

As for Robert, he went about his business. He seemed unconcerned with all the discussion, for he realized that only two days more remained for him.

He spent the afternoon and evening at home. After tea, the entire family gathered in the room where Clara lay. She was alive and breathing easily, but she was still unconscious. As Mary was saying something to her husband about his dream and the events of the day before, Clara suddenly opened her eyes and distinctly called out.

"Father, what day is it?" she asked.

It was like a voice out of the long-dead past.

Robert, sitting by the side of the bed, replied quietly, while his heart beat quickly. "This is Friday night, dear child."

Another question came, uttered in the same strange voice.

"Father, how many more days do you have left?" she said with more urgency.

Robert answered quietly, "Tomorrow and Sunday."

The voice came again. "I shall go with you then."

Her eyes closed and her body became motionless and limp as before.

Clara's words filled the family with dismay. Robert bowed his head and groaned. Mary, beside herself with grief, flew to the girl's side and tried to bring back to consciousness the mind that for a moment or two had gleamed with reason. The others, George and Will and Bess, grew pale, and Bess cried, almost for the first time since the strange week began.

Robert was the first to break the grief with a quiet word. He raised his head, saying, "I do not believe Clara is going to die when I do."

"Why do you think that, Father?" Alice asked.

"I'm not sure," he replied. "I can't give any exact reason. I only know that I don't believe it will happen."

"God grant that she may be spared!" said Mary. "Oh, Robert, it is more than I can bear. Only today and tomorrow left. I have battled against your dream all week. It was only a dream. I will not believe it to be anything else. You are not ill—there is no indication that you are going to die. I will not, I cannot, believe it. God is too good. And we need you now, Robert."

Robert shook his head sadly but firmly. "No, Mary. I can't resist an impression so strong that it has become conviction. I have struggled against it too, but it grows on me. God is merciful. I do not question His goodness. How much do I deserve even this week of preparation after the life I have lived? And the time will not be long before we shall all meet there."

The children drew about him lovingly. Bess climbed into his lap and laid her face against her father's, while the strong man sobbed as he thought of all the years of neglected affection in that family circle. The rest of the evening was spent in talking over the probable future.

George listened respectfully and even tearfully to his father's counsel concerning the direction of business and family matters. The young man was going through a struggle with himself, which was apparent to all in the house. Ever since his mother had seen him kneeling in the night watch, he had shown a new spirit.

Finally, the family gathered once again at Clara's bedside to pray. As the last member finished, a heavy silence seemed to envelope them all. It was very quiet in the room at the close of Robert Hardy's fifth day.

8.

SATURDAY

The Sixth Day

ROBERT COULD NOT believe that his seven days were almost at an end. It seemed just yesterday that he had dreamed after the Sunday evening service. As on every other day, he asked himself the question, "How best shall I use my remaining time?"

The day was spent in much the same way as the other days. He went down to his office about ten o'clock and, after coming home to lunch, went back again, with the intention of getting through all the business and returning home to spend the rest of the time with the family. Around three o'clock, when the routine work of the shops was completed, Robert felt an irresistible desire to speak to the men in his employ. Those in his department numbered about eight hundred, and he knew how impossible it would be for him to speak to them individually. He called Burns in and gave an order that made the foreman stare in the most undisguised wonder.

"Shut down the works for a little while and ask the men to get together in the big machine shop," Robert instructed. "I want to speak to them."

Burns had been astonished so often this week that, although he opened his mouth to say something, he was able to remain quiet. After staring blankly at his employer for a minute, he turned and went to carry out the order.

Robert crossed the yard from the office. He climbed onto one of the planing machines and looked about him. The air was still full of fumes, smoke, and the mixture of fine iron filings and oil that characterizes such places. The men were quiet and respectful. Many of them had heard their manager's speech of Thursday night at the town hall.

Most of them were aware that some change had taken place in him. It had been whispered about that he had arranged matters for the men injured in the Sunday accident so that they would not lack for financial support.

The grimy, hard-muscled crowd of eight hundred men all turned their eyes on the figure standing on the great planer. He in turn looked out through the blue murky atmosphere at them with an intensity of expression that none in the audience understood. As Robert went on with his speech, they began to understand what that look meant.

"My brothers," began Robert, with a slight tremble in the words so new to him, "as this may be the last time I shall ever speak to you, I want to say what I feel I owe to you. For twenty-five years, I have carried on the work in this place without any thought of the eight hundred men in these shops, except as their names were on the payroll of the company. It never made any difference to me when your wives and children grew sick. I never knew what sort of houses you lived in, except that in comparison with mine they must have been very crowded and uncomfortable. For all these twenty-five years, I have been as indifferent to you as a man possibly could be to men who work for him. It has not occurred to me during this time that I could be anything else. I have been too selfish to see my relation to you and act on it."

Some of the men coughed slightly or looked around awkwardly, unaccustomed to hearing Robert Hardy express himself with so much emotion.

"I might have been far more to you," he continued. "I might have spoken out, as a Christian and an influential director of this railroad, against the Sunday work and the harsh conditions here. I never did. I might have used my influence and my wealth to build healthy, comfortable homes for the men who work on this railroad. I didn't. I might have helped to make life a little happier and sweeter to the nearly one thousand souls in this building. But I went my selfish way. Yet for all that, I am no happier than any man here today."

Robert cleared his throat and continued, intent on concluding his speech with forthright clarity and conviction.

"Love God and obey him," he said in a strong, loud voice. "Don't envy the rich. They are often more miserable than you imagine. True happiness consists in a conscience at peace with God and a heart free from selfish desires. I thank you for your attention. You will know better why I have said all this to you when you come in here again to work next Monday. My brothers, God bless you."

When Robert stepped down from the planer and started toward the door, more than one hand was thrust into his with the words, "God bless you, sir!" His speech had made a profound impression on the men, and their response touched him deeply.

Robert went home. Everyone greeted him tenderly, and his first inquiry was about Clara's condition. She was still in that trancelike sleep. Mary had spent much of the day in prayer and tears. The evening sped by with the entire family gathered in Clara's room, talking quietly, reading passages from the Bible, and praying together.

James Caxton came and joined the family circle. His presence reminded Robert of his old quarrel with the young man's father. He said to James that if anything should prevent him from seeing his father the next day, James might tell him how completely and sincerely he wished the foolish quarrel forgotten and his own share in it forgiven.

So that day came to a close in tears, in fear and hope and anxiety and prayer. But Mary would not lose all hope. It did not seem to her possible that her husband could be called away the next night.

9.

SUNDAY

The Seventh Day

ও

LICE PLANNED THAT ALL the rest should go to church while she remained with Clara. Will was able to go out now. So, for the first time in months, Robert and his wife and Bess and the two boys sat together in the same church pew. George had not been to church for a year, and Will had been sporadic in his attendance.

The opening services seemed especially impressive

and beautiful to Robert. He wondered how he had ever dared sit and criticize Reverend Jones' preaching. Robert joined in the service with a joy unknown to him for years. He had come to it after reading his Bible instead of the morning paper, and after prayer instead of thoughts of his business.

Then the minister gave out the text for the morning's sermon: "For we must all appear before the judgment seat of Christ, that everyone may receive the things done in his body, according to that he hath done, whether it be good or bad."

Robert started, and leaned forward intently as the minister spoke, feeling that the message of the preacher was particularly for him.

"It is possible some soul is here today who for years has lived selfishly within his own little realm of pleasure," the pastor said. "He looks back on a life of uselessness, of neglect of all that Christ did for him. Today, he hears the voice of God. He listens; he repents; he cries out, 'God, be merciful to me!' What will God do? Will He reject him because he is a sinner, because he has wasted beautiful years? No! Is not God merciful? Let no man depart from this house of God fearful or despairing. The earthly life is full from beginning to end with the love of a Father."

Robert sighed deeply, comforted by Reverend Jones' words of grace.

"Men and women of Barton," the pastor continued, "you have heard the Word of God proclaimed from this pulpit today. No matter what age you are, or what circumstances you find yourself, there is time to seek God's forgiveness, mend broken relationships, and make peace with all. And as for you young men and women, will you wait until you are old to carefully assess your conduct of living? How do you know you will live to be old? Today is the day to make things right and change what needs to be changed."

Robert had many inquiries concerning himself and Clara to answer at the close of the service. He finally went up and thanked the minister for what he had said, and spoke as he had never spoken before in encouragement of his pastor's work. But he was anxious to return home. The time was growing short.

———————◆———————

At dusk, James came over and asked if he might join them. He did not know all that

Robert had gone through, but the children had told him enough to make him want to be with the family.

"Come right in and join the circle, James," Robert said cheerfully. "You're one of us."

So James drew up his chair, and the conversation continued. They were sitting in the room upstairs where Clara lay, facing an open fire. The doctor had called in the middle of the afternoon and brought two other skilled physicians at Robert's request. The doctors agreed it was a peculiar case and nothing special could be done.

When it grew dark, Alice started to turn on the lights, but her father said, "Let us sit in the firelight."

So the night passed. It was after eleven o'clock, and the conversation had almost ceased. All were sitting hushed in a growing silence, when Clara spoke again, so suddenly and clearly that they were all startled by it.

"Father! Mother! Where have I been?" she called out. "I have had such a dream! Where are you? Where am I?"

Mary rose and, with tears streaming down her face, knelt beside the bed. The girl came out of her strange unconsciousness with all her faculties intact. Gradually, she recalled the past, the accident, the dream of her father. She smiled happily at them all, and for a while they forgot the approach of midnight and its possible meaning to Robert. That is, everyone but Robert forgot. He knelt by the bed, at the side of his wife, and thanked God that Clara was restored.

———◆———

As the clock wound toward midnight, Robert looked at the faces of his family members gathered around him. How much he loved them—and how much he wished he had not squandered so many opportunities to express that love. Believing that his time was winding down, as surely as the clock's inner workings ticked away, he saw the contours of his life in sharp relief: The good things he had done, the selfish things he had done.... Most of all, he was thankful that God had given him a second chance—a chance for some small redemption. Suddenly, he rose to his feet and spoke aloud, quietly but clearly, "Did you hear that? Did you hear someone calling?"

His face was pale but peaceful. He bent down and kissed Clara, embraced his sons, drew his wife to him, and placed his hand on Bessie's head. Then, as if in answer to a command, he gently knelt again by his chair and, as his lips moved in prayer, the clock struck once more the hour of twelve. He continued kneeling there, nearer to God than he had ever been in all his life.

Thus Robert Hardy's seven days came to an end.

"*THUS* ROBERT HARDY'S SEVEN DAYS *CAME TO AN END.*"

❧

NYONE WHO FACES THE possibility of certain death surely undergoes a radical reordering of priorities. Charles Sheldon apparently left the ending of his story intentionally ambiguous, with the reader left to decide: Was Hardy called away that night by the voice he heard, or was it simply that the *old* Hardy died and the new one continued

on, "nearer to God than he had ever been" and transformed by the experience? We will never know for sure, but as the story encourages its readers to examine the way their faith works out in their priorities and actions, perhaps we, too, will be transformed in some small way by this book and others that Sheldon gave us.